DESERT KNIGHTS

Barry Cord

CHIVERS

THORNDIKE

This Large Print edition is published by BBC Audiobooks Ltd, Bath, England and by Thorndike Press®, Waterville, Maine, USA.

Published in 2003 in the U.K. by arrangement with the author c/o Golden West Literary Agency.

Published in 2003 in the U.S. by arrangement with Golden West Literary Agency.

U.K. Hardcover   ISBN 0–7540–7384–X (Chivers Large Print)
U.K. Softcover   ISBN 0–7540–7385–8 (Camden Large Print)
U.S. Softcover   ISBN 0–7862–5683–4 (Nightingale Series)

The text of this Large Print edition is unabridged.
Other aspects of the book may vary from the original edition.

Set in 16 pt. New Times Roman.

Printed in Great Britain on acid-free paper.

British Library Cataloguing in Publication Data available

Library of Congress Cataloging-in-Publication Data

Cord, Barry, 1913–
     Desert knights / by Barry Cord.
          p. cm.
     ISBN 0–7862–5683–4 (lg. print : sc : alk. paper)
     1. Illegal arms transfers—Fiction. 2. Large type books. I. Title.
PS3505.O6646D47 2003
813'.54—dc21   2003054009

707051

CHAPTER ONE

'It's this younger generation,' Windy Harris snorted. 'Smart alecks, all of 'em! If it wasn't for his maw, I'd give my nephew a hidin' when we find him. Hell, I always said the East spoils a man! Him an' his fool eddication—

'Hey!' he snapped in sudden alarm. 'Save me a swaller of that!'

The lanky man across from him took a deep pull at the bottle and passed it back across the campfire. Behind the two men the desert stretched dark and silent, its deceiving flatness broken on the north by the great bulk of Cimarron Peak. East and south the country slipped toward the Mexican border in a series of ragged, shadowy humps. High, puffy clouds blotted out areas of the starry sky, but over the eastern slopes an orange stain was spreading, heralding the late-rising moon.

'What did you say he was doin' out here?' Long Jim asked. He was eyeing the bottle tilted to Windy's lips and his question had only a bare interest behind it.

'Lookin' for rocks,' Windy snapped, lowering the bottle. 'Crazy job for a grown man, I sez. But his Maw claims that's what he studied at the college he went to. Calls it gee—gee-all—'

Long Jim reached across the fire and deftly

1

appropriated the bottle. Windy looked grieved. 'Hell, I was gonna save yuh some,' he said peevishly.

He picked up a piece of firewood and tossed it on the small blaze. 'Country's sure goin' to the dogs,' he muttered, and it was more than an idle remark.

Long Jim nodded. 'Ain't half the excitement used to be when I was a younker, Windy.' The lanky man had barely topped fifty—a long, lean, sinewy, saddle-toughened individual who ate like a horse and never gained an ounce more than his one-sixty.

'Now when I was a young feller—'

'You ain't dry behind the ears yet!' Windy jeered, appropriating the bottle again. He was a pint-sized man on the far side of fifty, with innocent blue eyes that could turn cold and hard. A ragged, peppery mustache gave his seamed face a square, stubborn look. But all in all he seemed harmless. He looked all of his years and a few more to boot, and the heavy, seven-inch barreled Colt .45 he wore on his right hip was usually taken as an old man's whim, to be disregarded. He and Long Jim had been saddle mates so long they had forgotten what it had been like before they had teamed up—a shiftless, humorous pair, they held no job longer than necessary to grubstake their wanderings.

Long Jim had settled back against his saddle. But Windy's remark brought him to his feet.

'Why, yuh ornery, chuckle-headed midget! For two cents Mex I'd—' He choked on the last word, as if it had gone down the wrong way. He was looking past Windy, toward the east.

Windy took a short, satisfied pull at the bottle. 'What happened?' he jeered. 'You swaller yore chaw?'

Long Jim's Adam's apple bobbed, but he couldn't get the words out. He gestured weakly toward the east.

Windy got up, the bottle held firmly in his hand, suspicion making him wary. He cast a quick glance behind him. The moon had come up over the eastern slope and it seemed balanced on the ragged crest like some lopsided orange. Against the moon's distorted face a bizarre creature was silhouetted—a long-necked, hump-backed monstrosity.

Windy gagged.

Behind this creature came another of the same breed. Only this one had a rider that bobbed loosely between the humps!

Windy shook the bottle, closed his eyes at the faint sloshing and tossed the bottle into the brush. He and Long Jim made simultaneous dives for their saddleguns. Long Jim came up first, working the lever of his Winchester. He drew a bead on the first of the strange apparitions and was squeezing the trigger when Windy deliberately jostled him.

3

The rifle spang startled the two-humped creatures. Their frightened snorts were distinctly audible in the desert stillness. Wheeling abruptly, they disappeared behind the slope.

Windy mumbled dazedly, 'I'm ropin' me one of them varmints, Jim. Even if I have to run it down to the gates of hell!'

He picked up his saddle and blanket and ran for his picketed horse. He saddled in record time and was aboard before Jim finished tugging at his cinches.

The dun mare took off like a startled jackrabbit as Windy jabbed his heels into her flanks. They took the slope at a run, and from the high ground Windy spotted the two strange animals running close together. But the one burdened with a rider was hampered by the jostling body and was falling behind.

Windy ran it down as it stumbled into a shallow wash. The half-pint oldster had shaken out a loop as he rode and he made a good underhand cast. The loop settled over the animal's head and in that moment Windy's cayuse, a trained cowhorse, planted its four feet stubbornly in the sand.

The rope whanged taut, the dun didn't budge, and the surprised camel somersaulted. Windy came down fast along his taut rope and sat on the dazed animal's flank.

'Reckon that'll hold yuh,' he muttered jubilantly.

4

But the camel had other ideas. Long Jim rode up as Windy struggled to keep the camel down.

'Trouble?' he queried unsympathetically.

'Dab a loop on the critter an' hogtie it!' Windy panted. 'Don't sit there like a—'

The camel rolled over, spilling the sawed-off oldster. It lunged to its knees, turned on the nearest object at hand and sank his teeth into Long Jim's chapped leg.

The big gray Long Jim was riding spooked and sunfished. Jim somersaulted out of saddle and landed spraddled on all fours with the angry camel breathing down his neck.

Windy intercepted it, trying to bulldog the animal to the ground. Long Jim went to his help and between them they managed to hogtie it.

Jim straightened and wiped his brow with a soiled neckerchief.

'Whew!' he grumbled. 'What kind of long-necked cayuse is that?'

'*Cayuse?*' Windy jeered. 'This is a camel, yuh chuckle-headed idjit!'

Long Jim scowled, hiding his ignorance. 'I know that,' he defended unreasonably. 'But what's the rider doin' roped between them humps?'

This had the effect he wanted. Windy turned his attention to the body—for the rider was obviously dead—and untied it.

The corpse was of medium build—a sandy-haired, mild-looking man in his late forties, Jim judged. He was wearing fawn-colored riding britches and a tan shirt of a cut not usually found along the Mexican border. He had been shot twice in the chest with a heavy-caliber gun, and probably not later than this morning.

Windy's eyes were a little hard. 'Someone around here has strange ideas when it comes to playin' a little joke, Jim. Maybe we should—'

'Whoa!' Long Jim interrupted hastily. 'Hold it, Windy! Reckon this is a job for the law in Goliath. We're just visitin' here, remember?'

Windy glanced at the hogtied camel. The animal snarled at them, exposing black gums and long, wicked-looking yellow teeth.

'Shore,' Windy said, nodding. His eyes were wide and innocent. 'I ain't lookin' for no trouble, Jim. Cripes, I'm just a peaceful old man—'

Long Jim's snort encompassed his entire opinion of his partner's avowed peacefulness.

'Come on,' he growled. 'Might as well get movin'. I ain't gonna get no sleep tonight, anyway.'

He limped back to his horse, grazing a few yards away.

'Better take care of that leg,' Windy advised, ' 'fore you get hydryphobia.'

He grinned at his partner's remark and looked up at the moon. It looked like the beginning of a promising weekend with his nephew.

CHAPTER TWO

Goliath had seen some strange things lately, so the appearance of what its citizens took for two saddle tramps leading a camel with a dead man dropped between its humps scarcely stirred them out of their dusty lethargy. A torpid somnolence gripped the town, a stupor attributed to the hot air that daily rose up to the benchland from the surrounding desert basin. Some town wags, however, were quick to point out that this was reversed in the evening, and that a lot of hot air flowed back from Goliath to the desert.

It was noon when Windy and Long Jim rode into Goliath, a huddle of shacks squatting like sunstruck prairie chickens in the hotbox that was known locally as Horsethief Gulch. A windmill at the end of town lifted water into a long, wooden trough for the consumption of all of Goliath's inhabitants, who used it sparingly, however, preferring the stronger bottled liquid hauled in daily from Bonesville, thirty miles north.

A straw-haired man with a star on his vest dozed in a chair in front of the law office. He looked up sleepily at the two strangers, straightened, and chewed vigorously on the straw between his thin lips. Turning his head, he called to someone inside the office.

7

'Hey, Chili! Come out here!'

A massive figure running mostly to stomach and jowls lumbered to the door. His star was pinned to a gravy-stained black vest, but so huge was his stomach that that symbol of law and order lay almost horizontal as he stood up.

He stared for a moment, blinking, scratching at the fringe of hair over his left ear and then observed without rancor, 'Coupla bums we're gonna have to run out of town, Jip.'

Windy and Long Jim were turning in toward the law office tiebar, their thoughts bothered by the dust and heat and mainly concerned with getting rid of their uncomplaining baggage.

The straw-haired man got to his feet as they rode up, gave a meaningful tug to his cartridge belt, and eyed the two riders with cool curiosity.

Windy leaned over his saddlehorn. 'You the sheriff of this flea-bitten town?'

'Mebbe,' the man aid. 'An' then again, mebbe not.'

Windy's eyes chilled. 'Now what kind of damn fool talk is that?'

The straw-haired man grinned insolently. 'I'm Jip Jenkins, pop. Depitty.' He jerked a thumb toward the fat man standing in the doorway. 'That's Chili Wetzler. Sheriff.'

Windy jerked a thumb over his shoulder. 'Wal, here's a hot job for yuh, Chili. Found this

8

jasper tied to that double-humped varmint an' we brung 'em both in.'

Chili took a long Mexican cheroot from his vest pocket and bit off a third. He chewed it like plug tobacco.

'What for?' he asked unconcernedly.

Windy scowled. 'Now that I've seen you an' yore deppity, I wonder. But it is customary in most parts of this country to bring a dead man in to the law. If you'll take a close look at the corpse, you'll find that he was shot—'

'Told the damn fool he'd git shot,' Chili interrupted placidly. 'Him an' that crazy gee-gee-allagist feller, Quincy Farrow.'

He turned and lumbered back into his office.

'Wait a minute, Coldspot!' Windy called after him. 'You can't—'

'He can—an' did,' Jenkins sneered. 'If I was you, pop, I'd get rid of that corpse in a hurry.'

Long Jim cut in before Windy's mounting rage found an answer. 'Who did the sheriff say was the other feller?'

'Nosy Easterner name of Quincy Farrow,' Jenkins growled. 'Lives in the Tolbert House, when he's in town. Spends most of his time out in the desert, though.' The deputy tapped his head significantly. 'Plumb loco, I say. This Farrow even brung in camels to pack supplies into the desert. Claims they're better'n mules—an' they don't need water.'

Long Jim was staring at Windy. 'Didn't you

9

say yore nephew's name was Farrow?'

Windy scratched his head. 'Damned if I didn't forget! Always called the button Red, but his maw used to git plumb riled. *Quincy!*' He snorted disgustedly. 'Ain't that a hell of a name for a man!'

Long Jim shrugged. 'If this corpse was a friend of his, mebbe we better let yore nephew take care of it.'

He turned to the deputy who was watching them out of narrowed eyes.

'Much obliged, Jip.'

The deputy watched them ride away. He chewed on his straw for a moment, his eyes hard.

'Might be a few more corpses floatin' around,' he muttered, ' 'for this week is over.'

*　　　*　　　*

The Tolbert House sagged with premature old age, the lines in its cracked adobe face resembling those of an old and wicked man. A well-dressed guest was sitting on thc shaded veranda, watching them, as Windy and Long Jim rode up.

He came to his feet and leaned over the low railing. 'Say!' he exclaimed, pointing to the body draped between the camel's humps. 'Ain't that William Sawyer?'

'Mebbe,' Windy retorted pugnaciously. After his encounter with the law he was

10

prepared for anything. But Long Jim took over.

'We're lookin' for a gent named Quincy Farrow. Heard he lived here.'

The guest smiled. 'My name's Paul Incalis. Publisher of the *Border Enquirer*. I know Quincy pretty well.' He tapped his temple with a stiff forefinger. 'Nice chap—but a little—well, peculiar, I'd say.'

He looked at Windy. 'Friend of yours?'

'Nephew. Haven't seen the squirt since I bought him a pony, nigh onto twenty years ago.' Windy frowned. 'His maw got plumb riled at me that time—as if a young 'un shouldn't learn early to fork a cayuse. 'Sides, he only busted his nose when he was thrown—'

Long Jim interrupted hastily. 'We found this corpse out on the desert, looped to this critter. Turns out he's a friend of Quincy's. We brung him in to the law, but no one there seemed interested.'

'Reckon the sheriff's got trouble enough with other things,' Incalis replied, 'to bother with a couple of damn fool Easterners. Begging your pardon,' he said, turning to Windy, 'seeing as how one of them is a relative of yours.'

Windy scowled. 'He might be a damn fool, but I wouldn't want to see him in this feller's condition. If anything happened to Red, I mean Quincy, my sister would never—'

'I know how you feel,' the publisher nodded.

'I tried to talk him out of prowling around out there. But—' Paul shrugged. 'Looks like El Porcito must have run into them. Lucky for Sawyer they only shot him.'

'El Porcito?'

'Yeah—the little pig. He's a Mex bandit who's been stirring up all sorts of hell just across the border. Makes his headquarters in Todoss por Niente, a Mexican town less than twenty miles from here.' Incalis shook his head. 'He's got a following among the border rabble and a big enough band of cutthroats to be taken seriously when he talks of a people's revolution.'

'What's all this got to do with that dead man?' Long Jim queried.

'El Porcito doesn't always stay on this side of the line,' Incalis explained. 'Right now he's Sheriff Wetzler's biggest headache—'

'That ain't the only thing big about the sheriff,' Windy growled. 'An' he shore seems to be takin' his job to heart.'

The sheriff's stentorian snores reached them all the way from the law office.

Paul Incalis was suddenly considerate. 'If you two don't mind, I'll take the responsibility for Bill Sawyer,' he said, indicating the body. 'I'll have him taken to Doc Meddle's—the doc does embalming on the side. I sure hope yore nephew ain't in trouble,' he added solicitously to Windy.

The older man frowned. 'Won't be the first

12

time,' he said. 'Much obliged to you for takin' this corpse off our hands.'

*   *   *

The inside of the Tolbert House sagged to the rear. The two dusty newcomers made their way around several potted palms that drooped their fronds in dry resignation, and found the desk clerk dozing behind the counter.

He was a pimply-faced boy with buckteeth and his pale eyes seemed to rattle around in his head as Windy pounded a fist on the counter.

'I'm Mr. Farrow's uncle,' Windy said. 'He in?'

'Ain't sure,' the clerk mumbled. 'He's in and out.' He turned and fished inside a pigeonhole behind him. 'Key's gone. Try Room 10, way down at the end of the hall. Upstairs,' he added as Jim and Windy turned away.

The door to Room 10 was closed but unlocked. Windy and Long Jim walked inside and the taller man said harshly, 'Wah!' The sun had been beating all morning through the east window and the small room was like a furnance. The lanky man walked to the window and flung it open. The glare from the street hurt his eyes and he turned quickly away.

Windy was eyeing the framed tintype of a sharpfaced woman on the dresser. 'Quincy's mother,' he grunted as Jim came up. 'This is his room, all right.' He turned and surveyed the small, faded, spartanly furnished cubicle, noting the black Gladstone bag at the foot of the iron-framed bed, the silver-backed comb-and-brush set on the stand below the cheap wall mirror.

He was turning for the door, growling, 'Let's get out of here, Jim,' when he caught a glimpse of a face outside the window. He turned quickly, jostling past his surprised partner and made a run for the opening. He got there in time to glimpse a slim, baggy-pants boy run across the flat roof less than three feet below the window, vault a low wooden parapet dividing this roof from another, and disappear.

Long Jim was shaking his head. 'Ain't any cooler out there,' he snapped irritably.

Windy didn't bother explaining. They went downstairs. The clerk straightened up as they approached.

'Tell Mr. Farrow his uncle's in town, when you see him,' Windy instructed him. 'We'll be back.'

The Red Bucket saloon was across the street and five buildings south. Windy and Long Jim mounted and rode the short distance to the hole-in-the-wall bar. Dismounting leisurely, they dropped reins over the pole bar and turned to the door.

Long Jim was leading by a stride when Windy glanced back to the Tolbert House.

14

The baggy-pants boy he had seen on the roof outside his nephew's window was just ducking in the hotel door.

He stopped. Jim glanced at him, frowning.

'Order me a beer,' Windy said. 'I'll be right back.'

He headed back for the hotel moving quickly and lightly for a man of his years. Jim watched him for a moment, then, used to the vagaries of his partner, he shoved his way through the batwings of the Red Bucket.

CHAPTER THREE

The desk clerk was nowhere in sight as Windy crossed the lobby and went upstairs, taking the steps two at a time.

He caught the Mexican boy in Quincy's room, going through his nephew's bag.

The youngster squirmed like a tomcat in the older man's grasp.

'Whoa!' Windy panted. 'Hold still, yuh light-fingered squirt!'

The boy made a final desperate try and nearly slipped free. Windy lunged after him and caught him just in front of the open window.

'Reckon I'll hafta tan yore brown hide—'

The voice in the doorway said with dry authority, 'No need, pop. I'll take him off yore hands.'

Windy turned his head. Jip Jenkins, the straw-haired deputy, was standing in the doorway, holding a Colt .45 rather carelessly in his right hand.

'Felipe needs a lesson in law-abiding manners,' he drawled. 'A night or two in the calaboose—'

The boy shrank back against the wall. 'No steal,' he said quickly to Windy. 'Me go now?'

'Not so fast,' Windy growled. 'What were you doing in here, if you wasn't stealing?'

'I look for letter. Mister Farrow say take letter to postmaster in Palmas, si!'

'Letter?' Windy frowned. 'What letter?'

'The kid's a natural-born liar,' Jenkins said harshly, coming toward them now. 'I've had him in the office a dozen times for stealing. This time I'm going to make the lesson stick!'

'Wait a minute!' Windy snapped. He turned to the frightened boy. 'Who did you say sent you?'

'Mister Farrow.' The boy's voice was sullen; he eyed Jenkins with apprehension.

'I'm camp boy for Mister Farrow and Sawyer. I ride to village for supplies. When I get back no Mister Sawyer. No Mister Farrow. I remember what Mister Farrow tell me. He say, "Felipe—if something happen to us, get letter from inside pocket of suitcase in my room and bring to Mister Neely, postmaster at Palmas." I think something happen to Mister Farrow and Sawyer. So I come to Goliath, like he say—'

Jenkins made a grab for the kid. 'He tells a slick story,' he rasped. 'Only I'm wondering if he didn't have a hand in what's happened. El Porcito's got more spies on this side of the border than there's flies around a slaughtered calf.'

Windy shrugged. 'Mebbe yo're right,' he said mildly. 'But the boy didn't take anythin', far's as I can make out. Leave him here. I'll talk to him—'

17

'If there's any talking to be done, I'll do it!' Jenkins snapped. There was an angry irritation in him now, brushing aside all pretense at good nature. He shouldered Windy out of the way and grabbed Felipe roughly by the arm.

'Come on you!' he snarled. 'I'll teach you to go around breaking into hotel rooms—'

Windy tapped him on the shoulder. Jenkins turned in annoyance and Windy jammed the muzzle of his long-barreled Colt into the deputy's midsection. Jenkins's face turned a lemon yellow. He started to gag and Windy laid the heavy weapon neatly across the top of his head.

The deputy collapsed without a sigh.

Felipe stared at the old reprobate with the wide brown eyes of a startled fawn.

Windy holstered his Colt, then knuckled the stubble on his chin.

'Suitcase you say?'

The boy nodded.

They searched the room, which was an easy task—there was no closet and only one small dresser. Some of Farrow's personal belongings were in the drawers. An old robe hung from a hook on the wall. There were some books on the night table, a battered alarm clock, some writing paper and envelopes in the table drawer.

They looked under the bed. A pair of scuffed slippers, but no suitcase.

Windy eyed the Boston bag the kid had

been going through. It held more books, a slide rule, triangle, a couple of notebooks and some chunks of ore-bearing rocks.

'Suitcase, eh? You sure?'

The boy nodded vigorously. 'That's what Mister Farrow said—'

The deputy began to stir.

Windy glanced at him, then turned back to the boy. 'You figger you can lead me to Mister Farrow's camp, son?'

Felipe nodded. He was plainly impressed by this old man's casual and easy handling of the straw-haired deputy who had quite a reputation in and around Goliath.

Windy put a hand on Felipe's shoulder. 'Well, let's get started.'

They went downstairs, brushing past a frowsy couple just ascending, and stepped out into the street. The sheriff's snores still rumbled reassuringly.

At the Red Bucket Windy said, 'Wait here,' and pushed through the batwings.

Long Jim was standing with one foot on the brass rail of the bar that held only one other half-potted customer. Three empty beer glasses made a triangle in front of him; Long Jim was lifting a fourth glass to his lips when Windy stopped by his side.

The grizzled bantam plucked the glass from his partner's hand, drained it and set it back carefully on the wet counter.

'Pay the gent,' Windy admonished quickly,

waving a hand to the scowling bartender coming toward them, 'and let's get out of here.'

Long Jim spluttered like a wet fuse. 'I'll be doggonned if I—'

But Windy had already left. Long Jim slapped a silver dollar on the bar and followed.

He didn't have time to ask questions. Windy was in his saddle with a Mexican boy riding up front, and he was holding the reins of Long Jim's horse in his left hand.

A door slammed down the street. Deputy Jenkins staggered out to the veranda of the Tolbert House, a gun in his fist. He looked as mean as a bear with a snoutful of bees.

'We better mosey along, Jim,' Windy advised calmly. 'The law in Goliath appears to be on a rampage.'

Jenkins' first shot spurred Long Jim's leap into saddle. Windy tossed him his reins and jabbed his heels into his mare's flanks. The deputy's wrathful yell curdled in the midday heat. His second shot broke a window just ahead of the fleeing oldsters.

Jim's voice raised angrily above the racket: 'What in tarnation did you stir up now?'

Windy only grinned.

*   *   *

The dun-colored hills caught the blazing heat of the late afternoon sun and made hot boxes

20

of the dry canyons through which the two riders moved. Their cayuses were tired. Felipe had alternated riding with Long Jim and Windy and he was back on Windy's dun mare, a slight, sharp-faced boy in a shirt three sizes too big and a tattered straw hat.

He stirred now, his eyes lighting up.

'There,' he said, pointing, 'in the canyon chico. There is the waterhole. Farrow and Sawyer, they make camp there—'

Windy squinted. Dust powdered his mustache and lay in the furrows of his neck and face. Unconsciously he rubbed his button nose.

'Hell of a place for a camp,' he growled.

The shack, faded a muddy gray under the beat of the border sun, clung like a wart on the side of the slope of the small feeder canyon. A lone, stunted tree and a bit of greenery marked the waterhole. Ocotillo and an occasional Joshua tree stood like sentinels on the slopes, guarding only they knew what.

They pulled up before the shack. The door was open and Windy knew that his nephew was not inside, but he dismounted anyway and entered while Long Jim and Felipe waited in saddle.

Some prior occupant, long since forgotten, had built this one-room dwelling of adobe and straw with laid branches, sealed with mud, for a roof. It had fallen into disrepair before Quincy and Farrow came upon it, for Windy

21

could make out signs of recent repair as he went inside.

The shack contained a variety of equipment which Windy assumed his nephew and Sawyer had used in their puttering around the hills: small picks, hammers, a scale, a wooden box containing jugs of chemicals. There was even canned food in a newly built cupboard.

Windy shook his head. He was thinking of his sister and of her letter which had decided him to ride down this way to look up a boy he had not seen in twenty years.

'—*keeps writing about you, John*—' (He was John to her, but he had been Windy so long that his proper name had an unfamiliar sound, as if she were writing to someone else.) '—*he thinks you're a character, whatever that means. But I'm not writing to remind you how much Quincy likes you—lately his letters have been guarded and I'm afraid he's involved in something dangerous*—'

He was not a hand at writing. Wryly Windy thought of the half-dozen letters he had mailed to Sarah in nearly twenty years. This one, telling her that Quincy was probably dead, would be the hardest.

He came outside and mounted behind Felipe, turning to look over the eroded slopes of the canyon.

Felipe shifted uncomfortably. 'Yesterday morning Mister Farrow send me to town for supplies. I come back pronto—no find him

22

here. Mister Sawyer, him gone, too. Betsy and General Grant—they gone—'

'*Who?*' asked Windy suspiciously.

'The camels,' the boy explained. 'Quincy name them.'

Long Jim shook his head. 'Looks like yore nephew inherited yore peculiar sense of humor,' he said to his partner. 'General Grant! Cripes!'

Felipe looked puzzled. Then he shrugged. 'I look for Mister Farrow. Up by the big montana someone shoot—' he fingered a hole in his hat. 'I wait no more. I remember what Mister Farrow say about the letter in his room—'

'What montana?' Windy interrupted.

Felipe turned in the saddle and pointed. 'That one. Someone shoot—bang! A good shot, señor.'

Windy's eyes were bleak. 'Let's take a look, Jim.'

They found nothing. No trace of Quincy, or of the rifleman Felipe swore had fired at him. Night found them tired, the horses drooping. They made a dry camp and went without grub, which Long Jim grumbled about until he fell asleep. Windy remembered the canned goods in the shack as he rolled up in his blanket. He should have had sense enough to bring some along, he thought, and fell asleep to dream of camels and canned foods and a fat sheriff who seemed to blow up in his face.

Long Jim was the first one up. Windy stirred

and looked at him, a crooked grin cracking his lips.

'Thinkin' of breakfast?'

'Ain't thought of nothing else,' the other confessed. 'Think we might find something in yore nephew's shack?'

Windy got to his feet. 'Wouldn't be surprised. I want to take another look around that canyon anyway.'

Felipe had built a small fire and was bunkered down in front of it. Windy said patiently, 'No sense in making that fire, son. We didn't pack any grub.'

He closed his mouth as Felipe pulled his hands out of his pants pocket and tossed something into the fire. The boy stepped back quickly. There was a sharp explosion, more like a .38 going off, and some of the embers scattered.

'What in hell . . . ?' Windy caught Felipe by the arm, his face grim. Long Jim had spun around, his Colt in his fist.

Felipe said, grinning, 'Mister Farrow give me these.' He thrust his hand into his pocket again and brought out a dozen loose firecrackers. 'Make plenty noise, huh?'

Long Jim choked. 'Firecrackers! Yore nephew gave him *firecrackers!*'

Windy shook his head. 'The damned fool. It ain't enough he has to come out here an' get mixed up in border trouble—he has to bring his own fireworks—' He caught himself, grinning despite himself at this facet of his nephew. Turning, he patted Felipe on the shoulder.

'All right, son,' he said gruffly. 'Save 'em for the Fourth. We're breaking camp.'

An hour later they rode down a brush-fringed gully and came within sight of his nephew's camp. The stillness had not been disturbed since they had left it. The late-morning heat was already unbearable.

While Long Jim ransacked the cupboard of canned food, Windy made another tour of the canyon. He found some tracks but he lost them on hard, scaly ground. In a sandy wash he came upon the imprints of a camel. Betsy? Or General Grant?

He remembered they had brought in Farrow's body on one of the camels—had Quincy ridden out of here on the other?

He went back to the shack. He ate a little of what Long Jim had prepared. Felipe watched both of them from over his plate of beans.

'You go back to town?' he asked, his mouth full. 'For letter for postmaster?'

Windy shook his head. 'We're going south.'

Long Jim looked up, surprised. 'South?'

Windy nodded. 'Mexico.' He looked at Felipe. 'You know where El Porcito hangs out?'

Felipe's eyes widened. 'El Porcito?' He made a quick gesture, drawing his fingers like a knife across his throat. 'It is very dangerous to see him, señor—'

Windy eyed the boy with narrowed gaze. 'Mebbe that straw-haired deputy back in town was right about you,' he said coldly. 'You trying to put us off?'

'No, no—' the boy protested. 'I will take you to San Juan—'

'San Juan?'

'Si.' The boy pointed. 'About ten miles, señor —just across the border. There you will find El Porcito.'

CHAPTER FOUR

San Juan dozed in the fierce midday sun. It lay a few miles below the Mexican line, straggling along the north bank of San Juan Creek, a watercourse that ran dry for most of the year.

It was an old village settled by Father Kino nearly two hundred years before when all of this vast and desolate land had belonged to the Indians, the Pimas and the Apaches. Spanish swords had conquered it and Jesuit priests had civilized it. The marks of both lingered in San Juan but were largely ignored by its inhabitants.

The old adobe church was badly in need of repair and the village priest was gone. Once a month a padre from Santa Luisa, fifty miles south, rode a donkey to San Juan and held mass, performed belated weddings and christened the babies born in the interval. He was a hardy man and he did not mind the journey, but he never left San Juan without praying for its inhabitants.

An old presidio looked down on the village from a hill across the creek. Over the years it had been used by Federales, bandits and revolutionaries, none of whom had remained long. It was falling slowly into ruin which did not displease San Juan's inhabitants who were ambivalent about the old brass cannon pointed down at the village from the fort which they alternately viewed as defending or threatening the village—it all depended on who occupied the presidio.

No one seemed to pay any attention to the strangers who came riding into town. It was siesta time, and even the flies were laying low.

An insomniac dog, a mongrel with so many crossed strains that the lines of breeding only served to confuse him, came out of an alley. He paused to stare at them for a moment, then gave a threatening bark. But his heart was not in it and he slunk back into the alley.

Felipe shifted nervously behind Long Jim. 'Señor,' he said uneasily, 'I have kept my word. Here is where you will find El Porcito—'

He started to slip out of saddle as he said this, but Long Jim reached behind him and grabbed a fistful of the boy's shirt.

'You just hang on, son,' he said grimly.

Riding alongside, Windy glanced at the boy. 'What you afraid of?'

Felipe licked his lips. 'El Porcito does not like strangers coming to San Juan—'

'Hell,' Windy said placidly, 'we don't aim to interfere with his revolution. All we want is to ask him a few questions—'

Windy paused as he saw the boy's face whiten. Up ahead a man came out of a building carrying a bucket of dirty water. He was a big man in dirty white camisa, sleeves rolled up past powerful, hairy forearms. He looked almost as wide as he was tall. He sloshed the contents into the dusty road, scratched himself sleepily and turned to go back inside, his gaze drifting idly to the approaching riders . . .

Felipe muttered, 'Tomas,' and slipped down from behind Long Jim before Jim could stop him. Windy jerked his cayuse around to head the boy off, but Felipe ducked quickly around him and disappeared into a nearby alley.

Up ahead Tomas bellowed, 'Felipe!' and started after him, swinging his wooden bucket menacingly.

Windy drew his Colt. He snapped, 'Hey!' as the big Mexican charged past him, yelling, 'Ladrone! Cabron!' The man ignored Windy and the gun and disappeared into the alley behind Felipe.

Long Jim grinned at his partner. 'Yuh sure made a big impression on him, Windy.'

The smaller man gave him a disgusted look and slipped his Colt back into his holster.

'Maybe he's deef,' Long Jim said.

'And blind, too?'

Long Jim glanced toward the alley. 'He sure was mad—'

He followed Windy as the smaller man rode to the mouth of the alley and looked inside.

The big Mexican was standing before a high fence at the end of the alley. He shook his fist at it, muttered something under his breath and came back toward the street, swinging his pail angrily.

Windy said, 'Jest a minnit, mister,' and swung his cayuse around to head the man off. Tomas paused, eyeing them. He seemed surprised to see then.

'What you got against that boy?' Windy asked.

The Mexican eyed Windy wrathfully for a moment, then shouldered Windy's horse aside and walked up the street, disappearing into the building he had come from.

Long Jim chuckled.

Windy turned on him, blue eyes snapping. 'Well, he ain't deef, an' he ain't blind!'

He patted the Colt snugged in the holster at his hip. 'Next time I'm gonna speak to him in a lingo he'll understand!'

Long Jim's gaze roamed across the dusty street and up the slope to the old Spanish fort. It looked deserted from here.

'The kid said we'd find El Porcito here,' he muttered. 'Let's go find out.'

The cantina into which Tomas had disappeared had a sign painted in black above the doorway: POR LOS REVOLUCIONE. Windy eyed it as he dismounted.

'Reckon we come to the right place,' he said as they went inside.

The thick adobe walls shut out the outside glare and most of the heat. Inside the cantina it was comparatively cool.

Long Jim and Windy paused by the door,

letting their eyes accustom to the change. There was the smell of cooking in the air—chili and beans and other things.

Long Jim sniffed happily. 'We've come to the right place,' he said and headed for the counter.

Windy hung back, eyeing the place, not trusting it. The cantina was just big enough to accommodate a half-dozen small tables. It had a recently swept earthen floor and a short counter. A door in back led into the kitchen.

A couple of Mexicans were dozing over a table in a corner. They stirred sleepily as Long Jim pounded on the counter, interest sifting into cold black eyes.

Tomas' voice was heard yelling in the kitchen. A girl's voice answered him. Windy knew just enough border Spanish to understand they were quarreling about the boy.

Windy joined Long Jim at the counter. Long Jim drew his Colt and fired a shot into the ceiling.

The quarreling in the kitchen stopped. After a moment a girl appeared in the doorway, angry and petulant.

She eyed them, hands on her hips. 'What you want, hah?'

She was perhaps twenty, olive-skinned and slim and full-busted, an attribute her low-cut peasant blouse displayed pleasingly.

Long Jim smiled disarmingly. 'Begging yore pardon, señorita—but me an' my partner are

31

starving. We haven't et since—'

'This morning,' Windy growled.

The girl switched off her angry look and flounced up to them, smiling.

'Oh . . . Americanos?'

'Yeah,' Windy said. 'From way up north—Montana.'

'Montana?' The girl's voice was soft and musical. 'Is that in America?'

Long Jim grinned. 'There's been some doubts about it, señorita—'

'Señora,' she corrected him. 'I have a husband.' A cross look came into her face. 'But he is a lazy, good-for-nothing peon who sits at home and dreams only of the revolution—'

'*Maria!*'

She stopped and looked at the big Mexican as he came to the doorway, but there was defiance in her eyes.

'Maria is the best cook in San Juan,' he said, coming toward them, 'but sometimes she talks too much. No?' He looked pointedly at her and she shrugged.

He went behind the counter. 'What'll you have, gentlemen? Beer? Pulque?'

Windy eyed the big Mexican suspiciously. 'I see the cat finally let go of yore tongue.'

Tomas eyed him, confused.

'Don't mind him,' Long Jim said. 'My partner gets a little delirious when he's starving—'

32

'Thirsty,' Windy cut in, growling. He had an eye on the two Mexicans in the corner and he didn't like the way they got up and left.

'Beer for both of us,' Long Jim ordered. 'And frijoles and enchiladas for me.' He looked at the girl. 'Double portion—and don't spare the chile, Maria.'

'Si,' the girl said. She headed them toward a table. 'I do not like the name Maria.' She giggled. 'All gringos call me Tony.'

She flounced off toward the kitchen.

Windy and Long Jim exchanged glances. They sat down and Tomas drew two glasses of warm beer from a tap. He brushed flies away with a homemade flyswatter and brought the beer to them.

Windy took a swallow of his. 'No ice?'

Tomas shook his head. 'They say it is bad for the blood, señor.'

He slapped viciously at a fly that lighted on the table in front of the small man.

'You are lost, perhaps?'

Long Jim shrugged. 'Not if this is San Juan. We're looking for El Porcito.'

Tomas scratched his head. 'You make fun of me, señor?'

Windy let his gun hand drop down to his hip. 'That boy you chased into the alley said El Porcito hung out here—'

The big man eyed them morosely, a spark of anger glinting in his eyes.

'Ah, Felipe! That boy, señors, is a liar and a

thief!'

'Could be.' Windy glanced at his partner, frowning. 'But he said we would find El Porcito here.'

Tomas sighed. 'You do not believe me? Ask her.' He nodded toward Maria coming out of the kitchen with a plate heaped high with beans and enchiladas.

'Ask me what?' she demanded suspiciously. Then, before anyone could speak: 'I'll have you know I am an honest married woman—'

'About Felipe,' Tomas cut her off.

The girl eyed the two norte americanos angrily. 'You know my brother?'

'I'd like to get my hands on him,' Windy growled.

'You see,' Tomas said, 'you are mistaken. There is no El Porcito here.'

Windy frowned. 'Up in that old fort on the hill, perhaps?'

Tomas's eyes lidded. 'There is no one there,' he assured them. 'Many years ago the Federales—' He shrugged. 'But now . . . only goats, señors.'

'But you've heard of El Porcito?'

'Everybody has heard.' Tomas made a broad gesture of disbelief. 'But . . . no one pays attention—'

'That sign over yore door—For the Revolution?'

'Painted by some misguided soul,' Tomas replied. He sighed heavily. 'There is no El

Porcito here. And as for the revolution—' He shrugged huge shoulders. 'It is a dream in Mexico, nothing more.'

He walked back behind the counter and slapped viciously at flies gathered around a wet spot.

The girl was staring at them, hands on her hips. 'My brother,' she said sharply, 'he came to San Juan with you?'

Long Jim nodded.

'He steal from you?'

'We haven't checked everything out yet,' Windy growled.

'He is a wild boy,' she said, 'and he does not always tell the truth. But he is my brother. I will not have anyone hurt him.'

She gave Tomas a defiant, angry look and flounced back into the kitchen.

Windy sipped his unpalatable beer and watched Long Jim devour his meal. Tomas eyed them morosely from behind the counter.

Maria slammed a few pots and pans around in the kitchen, and then it was quiet. Outside it was hot and still. The buzzing of flies was loud and clear, interrupted occasionally by the flat hard sound of Tomas' flyswatter.

The sound came from some distance off— an odd, harsh braying.

Windy glanced at his partner, but Long Jim was too busy eating.

The sound was not repeated.

Long Jim finished and pushed his empty

plate away. 'Don't see how you do it,' he told Windy. 'Some day yo're just gonna dry up and blow away.'

Windy grinned. 'I get stuffed jest looking at you eat.'

They paid Tomas for the meal and the beer and left a small tip for Maria.

'For the revolution,' Windy said, and they went out.

CHAPTER FIVE

The street lay still and deserted in the afternoon heat. The cottonwoods drooped over San Juan Creek. Up on the hill the old brass cannon poked its muzzle through a break in the adobe wall, a useless reminder of other days.

Long Jim glanced up at it. 'Let's take a pasear up to that old fort,' he suggested.

'What for? Ain't nothing up there.'

Long Jim shrugged. 'Won't hurt to look. Felipe said we'd find him here.'

'You heard his sister,' Windy grumbled. 'Even she doesn't believe him.' He glanced back up the street. 'Scatted first chance he got.' He shook his fist in the direction of the alley. 'If I git to lay my hands on that boy again, I'll—'

He paused, eyes narrowing.

'You hear it, Jim?'

Long Jim frowned. 'What?'

'Sounded like a mule braying . . . or a jackass—'

The sound came again, ululating over the drowsy, quiet street.

'It ain't a jackass,' Long Jim said definitely, 'an' it ain't a mule—'

The camel came padding into view then, emerging from some backyard. Someone had tied the animal with an old rope and it had broken loose. A length of it trailed in the dust behind it.

It came padding disconsolately toward them, bizarre humps bobbing, long neck dipping in a sort of loose L. Then it spotted the two men by the cantina and a gleam came into the camel's eyes. It gave off with a raucous greeting and headed for them.

Long Jim backed away, fending off the animal with an upflung arm.

Windy yelped, 'Hey!' as a long black tongue licked across his face. He took off his hat and batted at the camel. 'Get away from me, yuh miserable excuse for a cayuse!'

The camel eyed him with sad and disconsolate gaze. Long Jim said, 'Wait a minnt, Windy.' He moved in on the camel. 'Betsy?'

The camel swung around to him and started licking him with great affection.

Long Jim shoved her away. 'All right, all right,' he growled. 'I ain't a salt lick.'

He turned to Windy. 'She answers to Betsy. That means yore nephew must be around here somewhere.' Windy grasped the length of halter rope and studied the frayed end. 'Broke loose—'

'Leave him alone, señor!' a man's voice interrupted coldly.

They turned to look as a tall, easy-walking Mexican came toward them. He was a young, ruggedly handsome man with quiet, intelligent eyes. He wore a serape over his shoulder and a gun on his hip, but the rifle in his hand was old and its cracked stock was held together with rawhide.

'I will take care of him,' he said, coming up. He had just a trace of accent.

Windy checked him over coldly. 'You say it's yores?'

The man nodded. 'Raised him from a colt. An ungracious animal, señor.' He grabbed the halter rope and gave it a yank. 'Borrachone!' he snarled in Spanish. 'I will teach you to—'

The animal jerked back, baring big yellow teeth. The Mexican gave him another yank and this time the camel went for him, knocking him down. The man's rifle went off, chipping adobe from the cantina wall.

The man tried to scramble to his feet . . . and the camel sank its teeth into his shoulder.

Windy glanced at Long Jim; the stringbean grinned. The Mexican was yelling in alarm and beating his fist against the camel's nose.

Long Jim pulled the camel away. 'That's enough, Betsy.' He shrugged as the camel gave a loud raucous sound of distaste. 'Don't blame yuh none.'

The man scrambled to his feet and went for his rifle, blood in his eye. Windy planted his boot on it before the man could pick it up. The oldster jammed his Colt under the Mexican's nose as the other backed off and went for his gun.

The self-proclaimed camel-owner stared at the big gun in Windy's fist, a tightness around his mouth.

'Ah,' he said thickly, 'you are a camel thief, eh?'

'Ramon!'

The man turned to face the girl who had come to the cantina doorway. Maria stood with her hands on her hips. 'I see you are making a fool of yourself again, hah?'

Ramon said bitterly, 'I do not wish to speak with you,' and turned on his heel to go.

'Wait a minnit!' The sharpness in Windy's tone held Ramon. Windy shot a look to Maria. 'Who is he?'

'My husband,' Maria sneered. 'The one who dreams of revolution.'

'Looks to me like he's been doing a bit more than dreaming,' Windy said grimly. He eyed Ramon. 'Where'ud you get that animal?'

'I told you,' Ramon answered sullenly.

'Whatever he told you, don't believe him,' Maria broke in. 'He is a liar, like my brother.'

'Said he raised him from a pup,' Windy said.

'Colt,' Long Jim corrected.

'I found him wandering around out there—' Ramon waved vaguely. 'I thought . . . what a strange animal . . . must be valuable. So . . . I brought him here to my home, señor. I have never seen anything like him. I feed him . . . give him water. But is he grateful—'

'It's a she,' Windy cut in drily.

Ramon paused. 'I didn't look,' he admitted. He shrugged, then made a magnificent gesture of sacrifice. 'You want him, señor? You will pay?'

'We want her,' Windy said. 'And we'll pay. But not for Betsy.'

Ramon frowned. 'Betsy?'

Maria said quickly, 'For what will you pay?'

'Information.' Windy backed toward her, keeping his eye on Ramon. Long Jim seemed to have his hands full keeping the affectionate Betsy away from him.

'I want to find out what happened to a man named Quincy Farrow.'

Ramon stiffened and licked his lips.

Maria's voice changed. For the first time there was a thread of fear in it.

'You are looking for Señor Farrow?'

Windy nodded. 'He came here?'

'Two days ago.' Maria licked her lips. 'He wanted to see El Generale—'

'Maria!' Racoon's voice was sharp.

Windy moved up to her. She was standing to one side of the door now, hestitant, her defiance crumbling.

'What do you know about Farrow?' His voice was rough.

'Nothing. He was here . . . that's all I know—'

'Who is El Generale?'

Maria's gaze darted to Ramon. He was

41

eyeing her coldly.

'Look,' Windy told her grimly, 'we don't give a hang what's going on down here. All I want is to find Farrow—'

He heard the step behind him but he did not get around in time. Tomas's shotgun barrel came down across his head, crumpling his hat.

Windy sagged and fell forward. Long Jim let go the halter rope and swung around, but paused as Tomas slanted the ugly muzzle toward him.

'Señor,' a thin, reedy voice said. 'I hear you are looking for me.'

Long Jim dropped his hand by his side and turned. A half-dozen riders came out of the alley behind him, fanning slowly across the street. They were dusty, hard-faced men with bandoliers slung across their shoulders.

The man on the big white horse was wearing a Spanish officer's gaudy tunic and plumed hat. The plume drooped and the gold braid was tarnished, but he rode like a man who commanded a regiment. He was short and round-faced and his eyes had a sad, faraway look. Across his saddle, gagged and squirming, was Felipe!

The man rode slowly toward the cantina to pull up alongside Ramon. His gaze slid over Windy's unconscious form and held on Long Jim.

'I am El Porcito,' he said. His voice was too thin, too reedy for command . . . yet there was something about him that commanded respect. A dedication, perhaps—a genuine feeling for his country.

His lips twisted slightly. 'At least, that's what the gringos call me, señor.'

Maria ran to her brother's side. 'Generale,' she pleaded, 'please? He is only a boy—'

'He is an informer, a friend of the gringos,' the Mexican revolutionary said. 'I warned him.'

'What will you do with him?'

'He will be shot,' El Porcito said, 'like these two.'

'No . . . no—' Maria clutched at him. 'I will answer for him, Generale . . . I will . . .'

He shoved her away and looked at Ramon. 'She is your responsibility! Take her away!'

Ramon moved toward her. Maria backed off. 'Don't you touch me!' She turned toward the Mexican leader. 'El Generale!' She spat. 'El Porcito fits you better. You . . . with your talk of revolution . . . you make war instead on small boys and old men—'

El Porcito's face hardened. 'Ramon!'

Ramon clamped a hand over his wife's mouth. She tried to bite him. He held her tightly.

'She is a cross to bear,' Ramon muttered. 'But she is a woman—'

'With a loose tongue,' El Porcito said coldly. He raised his right arm and the riders behind him came up, flanking him.

He motioned to Windy and Long Jim. 'Bring them along!' He turned his big white stallion and without another look at the scene he rode across the street and headed up the slope toward the old fort.

CHAPTER SIX

Windy stirred. He sat up and ran his fingers through his hair and grimaced as they came in contact with the lump on his head. There was a sharp throbbing pain over his eyes and his vision was blurred.

He closed his eyes again. 'Jim . . . ?'

A snore answered him.

He kept his eyes squeezed shut, thinking. The last thing he remembered was Maria, the frightened look in her eyes . . .

Wood joints creaked under him as he slid a hand down to his side, feeling a plank support under him. His hand brushed against his holster. He was not too surprised to find it empty.

He opened his eyes. He could see an old oak beam, hand-hewn and warped, a few inches above him, supporting a crumbling ceiling.

He saw now that he was on the upper of two bunks set against the back wall of what appeared to be an old Army guardhouse. There were bars set in the window in the wall and the small square opening in the plank door was also barred.

He swung his boots over the side and gingerly let himself down to the floor. Long Jim's snoring seesawed across the room.

45

Windy ran his fingers through his hair again, feeling peevishly irritated at his partner's apparent unconcern.

He reached over and shook Long Jim roughly. Jim bolted upright, cracking his head on the bottom of the upper bunk.

'Jesus Christ!' Long Jim glared at Windy as he rubbed his head.

Windy looked around. 'What in hell happened?'

'Yuh got slugged!' Long Jim snapped. 'I got tired of waiting for yuh to come around.'

Windy sank down on the bunk beside the stringbean. 'Where are we?'

'In jail.' Long Jim walked to the door and motioned Windy to join him.

'Take a look.'

Windy came up and peered through the barred opening. The sun had gone down behind the adobe walls of the parade ground, leaving a pinkish glow in the sky. Much of the old fort had gone to ruin, but Windy could see a long adobe barracks building that appeared to have been recently repaired and, apart from it, what had been officer's quarters. A small flag flew over the headquarters building—a green and red flag with a clenched fist embroidered into it.

Windy swung around to his partner. 'Reckon the kid wasn't lying, after all. Looks like El Porcito's headquarters to me.'

Long Jim nodded. He was standing by the

46

wide window, looking out. He could see across this corner of the parade ground to the old brass cannon poking through a break in the wall. Closer and at a point where the wall was intact and higher, three posts had been driven into the ground. They had been there a long time—and the wall behind them was pockmarked by bullets.

Windy crossed to Long Jim's side and peered out. A small figure was tied to the center post. He hung limply, head down.

Windy jerked his head around to his partner. 'Looks like Felipe.'

'It is,' Long Jim answered grimly. 'They're gonna shoot him in the morning. At sunrise.'

Windy eyed him. 'Aw, come on, Jim. He's only a boy.'

'That's what El Generale said.'

'El Generale?'

'That's what they call him here. Seems like he doesn't like the name El Porcito.'

'Can't say I blame him,' Windy muttered. He stared across the parade ground to the boy. He was too far away to see the boy's face. A guard squatted by an old carreta, smoking, his rifle propped up against the wheel.

'They hurt the kid?' There was a tightening anger in the little man's voice.

Long Jim shrugged. 'Don't think so.'

Windy walked back to the bunk and sat down. His head ached, but he knew he'd get over it. He found his hat on the floor and put it on. His palm swung down again across his empty holster and he swore softly.

'Kinda feel responsible for the boy,' he said. 'We got him into this, making him take us to San Juan—'

'Not much we can do,' Long Jim growled. He remained by the window, looking out. 'We'll be lucky if we don't join him.'

He turned to eye his partner. 'Pretty scroungy-looking outfit, from what I've seen. Can't be more than a half-dozen men here, including El Porcito. Half of them don't have guns.' He shook his head. 'Can't figger out why that newspaperman, Paul Incalis, was so hepped up about them—'

'Hell with Paul Incalis!' Windy growled. 'I'm wondering how my nephew got mixed up in this. Young fool should'a' stayed back East, where he belonged.'

He scowled as Long Jim held up a warning hand.

'Looks like we're gonna have company,' Long Jim said.

The two men came to the guardhouse and one of them unlocked the door. They were swarthy, hard-looking men. One of them carried a rifle, the other held a machete. Of the two, the machete looked the more dangerous.

The man with the rifle leveled it at Long Jim. The other crossed to Windy.

'El Generale wishes to speak to you.'

They went out, crossing the parade ground to the headquarters building. Windy glanced across the parade ground to the boy, but it was already getting dark and he barely made out the small figure tied to the execution post.

There was a light burning in El Porcito's office. The small Mexican revolutionary leader was standing behind his desk, next to an old wall map of the province of Chihuahua. There was a circle drawn about the province capital and two converging lines, like arrows leaving San Juan and aimed at Goliath across the border.

There was also a small circle around a peak called El Rojo Montana on the map, but it was across the Mexican line and some miles southeast of Goliath. Windy, eyeing it, guessed it had some special significance for El Porcito.

Ramon was standing to one side, a sullenly silent and angry man. The two guards took up positions by the door.

El Porcito studied them for a moment. He looked like a comic opera general, except that he was deadly serious. He was holding a saber with which he had been pointing to the wall map. He tapped his boot side with it, letting them wait. Then:

'What were you doing in San Juan?'

Long Jim started to answer, but Windy headed him off. 'Prospecting, El Generale.'

El Porcito frowned. 'There is no gold here.'

Windy shrugged.

'That boy, Felipe—where did you meet him?'

'In Goliath.'

'Ah!' El Porcito glanced coldly at Ramon. 'They admit the boy brought them here, Ramon—'

'He didn't want to come,' Windy intervened. 'We kinda forced him to.'

El Porcito stared at them for a moment, then sank into the chair behind his desk. He began to clean his nails with the point of his saber.

'Look,' Windy said, moving toward him, 'like I said we're just two old prospectors poking around this part of the country. We stopped in Goliath to look up my nephew, Quincy Farrow—'

El Porcito sat up stiffly. 'Ah, yes—Farrow!' His eyes narrowed. 'Is that why you had Felipe bring you here?'

'We thought you might know what happened to him?'

El Porcito smiled.

'We heard some pretty scary stories about you in Goliath,' Windy went on. 'We figgered Quincy might have gotten himself in trouble over here.'

El Porcito tapped his boot with the flat part of his saber. 'What was your nephew doing in Goliath, old one?'

Windy glanced at Long Jim. 'Far as we know he was working for the government—'

'The United States Government?' El Porcito bounced to his feet, waving his sword at Windy. 'Meddling in the internal affairs of another country is treason, señor!'

'I don't know if he was meddling in anything!' Windy snapped. 'His mother said he was down here looking for rocks.'

'A likely story,' El Porcito sneered.

Windy sucked in a harsh breath. 'If he's in trouble here, let me talk to him?'

'Señor Farrow is not here,' El Porcito said coldly. 'But I assure you, if he comes to San Juan again, he'll be shot—'

'Like you shot his partner, Bill Sawyer?'

El Porcito frowned. 'Señor Sawyer is dead?' He seemed genuinely surprised.

'We found his body strapped to a camel a few miles out of Goliath.'

'I had nothing to do with that.' El Porcito was silent a moment, his eyes sad. 'I cannot be concerned with what has happened to Señor Sawyer and Farrow. I have my people to think of—' He made a gesture to the wall map. 'A thousand small villages scattered over the high desert . . . men and women and children living and dying with empty bellies. The village priests say they should have faith in God. But the government soldiers come and tax them so they have nothing left. Those who protest are shot—'

He was silent again, a small man in a soiled and faded uniform.

51

'Some day it will all change,' he said. 'Some day the people of Chihuahua will find a man who will lead them out of their slavery—'

'You?'

El Porcito fixed Windy with a sad and bitter stare. 'If not me, someone else. It is inevitable.'

'Raiding towns across the border won't help,' Long Jim muttered.

'I have no choice,' El Porcito snapped. 'I need guns, ammunition, powder. Where will I find them? In the poor villages of my people?'

He settled into the chair behind his desk, his eyes brooding. 'I am sorry, señors, you came here. I do not know where Mister Farrow is. He is not my problem.'

'That camel,' Windy said, swinging around to face Ramon. 'Mebbe he knows more—'

'Enough!' El Porcito cut in harshly. 'We have talked enough.' His fingers tightened around the hilt of his saber. 'I know what I am to the gringos across the border. A joke, señors! El Porcito—the little pig! Well, they shall see—'

He made an abrupt gesture to the guards. 'Take them away. Tie them to the execution posts. We will shoot them in the morning!'

'Hey! Wait a minnit!' Long Jim backed away from the advancing guards, turned to El Porcito. 'In my country a man usually gets a trial.'

'This is not your country!' El Porcito snapped. 'No one invited you here.'

The two guards closed in. The one with the machete smiled wickedly.

'You wish to protest, señor?'

Long Jim shrugged. 'Not without a lawyer—'

The man shoved him toward the door. Windy followed. They went out, the guards falling in behind them.

CHAPTER SEVEN

Ramon waited until they had gone. Then he walked slowly to the desk, a tall and disturbed young man, and looked down on the Mexican leader.

'The boy,' Ramon said quietly, 'I promised Maria. Let him go. We will keep an eye on him.'

El Porcito shook his head. 'It is too risky, Ramon. At this time, especially.'

'You will shoot him?'

El Porcito smiled. 'I am not a monster, Ramon. But letting him spend the night out there, thinking so, may put the fear of the devil in him.'

Ramon sighed. 'He has been frightened enough, Generale. Turn him loose. I will be responsible for him.'

El Porcito shook his head. 'I do not trust him, Ramon—'

'He is a liar and sometimes a thief,' Ramon admitted. 'But . . . maybe it's my fault, too. He is too much for Maria to handle, and I—'

'He is friendly with the gringos,' El Porcito snapped. 'How do I know what he told them?'

Ramon frowned. 'You heard what they said, those two. Bill Sawyer is dead. Perhaps Farrow is, too.'

The little Mexican got up and began to

54

pace.

'I promised Maria I'd bring him home,' Ramon pressed. 'And you know my wife.'

'Who in San Juan doesn't?' El Porcito paused, eyeing Ramon, a displeased look on his face. 'She is a troublemaker.'

Ramon nodded. 'It is the cross I have to bear.'

'How can you care for that woman? She calls you lazy and good for nothing. She tells this to anyone in San Juan who will listen.'

Racoon's lips twisted in a hurt, wry smile. 'It is because I understand her, Generale. She is a practical woman. She does not believe in the revolution. And she does not dream of tomorrow, like I do. She lives only for today.'

'And you?'

Ramon placed his hands on the desktop and stared across it to the smaller man. His voice was soft. 'I've known you when you were a boy, Zolo—before you became El Generale. You know how I feel about this revolution. How I feel about you.' He paused, his gaze locking with El Porcito's. 'But if you hurt that boy—'

El Porcito stiffened, anger in his eyes. Then it passed and he sighed. 'I need you, Ramon. You are my right hand.'

He paced again for a moment, then turned and nodded. 'All right,' he said, 'you can have the boy.'

Ramon straightened.

'On one condition,' El Porcito added coldly.

'That you keep him tied up, until after our raid on Goliath.'

Ramon nodded. 'I'll see to it.'

Ramon crossed the darkening parade ground, feeling the evening's cooler breeze against his face. It was the best time of day, he thought, when the harsh glare of the sun had gone and a certain peace crept in with the lengthening shadows.

He thought of Maria and he knew he had been neglecting her. It was partially his fault she was known as the wagging tongue of San Juan. But he knew and appreciated her other qualities, not all of them physical. Beneath that sharp-tongued exterior was a generous and warm-hearted woman.

He paused in front of the execution posts. The guard, Celestino, was a small, wizened man past the age of hard riding. He was hunkered down beside the carreta, a broken-down two-wheeled vehicle long abandoned, bleaching in the harsh border sun. An old muzzle loader was draped across his knees.

Guns and ammunition, Ramon thought . . . what could they do if they had enough of these? Take over all of Chihuahua, at least . . . a thousand men would spring up behind El Generale, if he could promise this.

Celestino rose. 'They have been very quiet, Ramon.'

Ramon eyed Felipe. Windy and Long Jim were sitting on the ground, their hands tied around the post in back. It was the most comfortable position possible, under the circumstances.

'Cut the boy loose,' Ramon ordered.

Celestino stared at him, mouth dropping. A pair of snaggly teeth showed. 'But . . . El Generale—'

'The boy!' Ramon snapped.

Celestino stared dubiously toward the headquarters building. 'I have orders—'

Ramon dropped his hand to his holster gun. 'Do you wish to question mine, old man?'

'No, no—' Celestino mumbled. 'If you will take the responsibility—'

'*Cut him loose!*'

The old man drew a knife from a sheath at his side and cut Felipe's bonds. The boy rubbed his hands together; he smiled uncertainly at his brother-in-law, not quite sure what Ramon was up to.

'Come on,' Ramon said. 'I'm taking you home.'

The boy looked down at the two oldsters. 'And them?'

'They are no concern of yours,' Ramon said coldly. 'Or mine.'

The boy hesitated. 'They have done nothing, Ramon. They come here looking for Mister Farrow, that's all—'

Ramon glanced back to the headquarters building, 'Perhaps you wish to stay here with them, then?'

Felipe licked his lips. 'They will be shot?'

'In the morning.'

Long Jim said quietly, 'Thanks, kid. But you better get going before he changes his mind.'

Windy grinned. 'Sure, kid. You don't owe us anything.'

The boy nodded. 'I tell Mister Farrow when I—'

'You will tell no one anything!' Ramon snapped. 'I will see to that!' He grabbed Felipe roughly by the arm. 'If it was not for Maria I would leave you here with them!'

CHAPTER EIGHT

The moon rose over San Juan, brushing a soft light over the old adobes. Old ghosts came out to dance in the shadows—ghosts of older and better days when this land was young and the Pimas and the Zunis who made their peace with the Jesuit priests, helped to fight off the marauding Apaches who never had.

It was a long way from Chihuahua, the capital of this Mexican province, and even further away from Mexico City. For most of the year the village was forgotten by the officials residing there. But lately there had been rumors circulating in San Juan that the Federales would be coming this way, curious about the stories seeping back to Chihuahua about a bandit leader—their assessment—named El Generale.

These rumors the people of San Juan discounted. But more immediate and disturbing was the edge of fear that began to occupy their days . . . the fear that the gringos across the border world soon retaliate for El Generale's indiscretions.

The moonlight stole through the small window and into the tiny room where Felipe lay, his bands tied securely to the brass bedposts. It was an uncomfortable way to sleep, and Maria had argued against such 'barbarity to a small boy,' but Ramon had coldly insisted. He did not wish to spend the night standing watch in Felipe's room—or, he had eyed her, was this what she wanted?

Faced with this choice, Maria relented.

The house was quiet now. Maria and Ramon were asleep. It was well past midnight, how long past Felipe could only guess.

He kept thinking of the two men tied up in the old presidio. El Generale was going to have them shot in the morning. Why should he care?

Felipe had lived most of his lifetime by his wits. He owed nothing to anyone, not even his sister.

But he kept remembering that the little man called Windy had stopped the deputy in Goliath from taking him to jail. And he was the uncle of Señor Farrow . . .

His wrists were numb. Slowly, carefully, he curled his legs up over his head. The bed creaked and he paused, listening. The snoring in the other room was soft and unbroken.

He curled his feet over the brass headboard and pushed gently against the wall. The back of his neck ached and his wrists hurt. But the bed moved slowly away from the wall. He let his feet down again, biting back the pain. In the other room his sister and Ramon slept like logs.

He waited until the strain in him eased, then he curled his feet up again, over the low headboard, resting his lean stomach on it for a moment, feeling the iron crossbar bite into skin. He swiveled his wrists around inside the rope and slowly eased himself down between the wall and the bed.

He was facing the headboard now, and by straining he could reach his left wrist with his teeth. It was slow, hard work, for Ramon had done a good job. But eventually he loosened the knot and his small-boned hand slipped free.

It took but a moment to free his other hand.

He stood quietly, listening. He had grown up here, with Maria, after his father and mother died. He did not remember them. But from the day he was old enough to think such things, he knew he did not like to stay in San Juan.

He slipped noiselessly past his sister's bedroom and out the door, turning on bare feet, carrying his sandals, to the backyard.

There was a small, makeshift shed in back of the house. Betsy raised her head and eyed Felipe as he came up. She started to snicker, but he raised a finger to his lips and said, 'Shhhhh' and, strangely, she obeyed.

He untied the ungainly animal.

'Kneel.'

The animal went down, folding her forelegs under her. He swung up between the humps and she heaved erect. Felipe guided her by a touch on the side of her neck.

They stole out of the backyard, the camel padding quietly on wide-splayed feet. The stars gleamed brightly over San Juan, a thousand tiny pinpricks in a velvet sky.

They crossed San Juan Creek and went up the slope. The presidio, Felipe knew, was not guarded. Only a handful of men stayed there with El Porcito. The rest slept with their women in the village.

He knew the presidio as well as he knew his backyard—he had played soldier there many times before El Porcito had come to make his headquarters here.

He pulled to a stop a few yards from the adobe wall and tied Betsy securely to a mesquite bush.

'Be quiet,' he admonished. The camel nipped playfully at him and fell to chewing on the tough mesquite leaves.

He crawled to the wall and slipped along it to a break just beyond, then looked across the parade ground. He was at a point not too far from where Windy and Long Jim sat with their backs against the posts. They seemcd to be dozing.

El Porcito was asleep in his quarters. Perhaps three or four men slept in the ruined barracks.

Felipe ran a finger down the side of his nose, thinking. He searched for and found the old man, Celestino, asleep in the carreta.

Felipe pulled back from the opening in the

wall and circled noiselessly as a prowling coyote, coming up behind the stables. He slipped inside and froze as El Porcito's white stallion snorted nervously.

He waited until he could make out Long Jim's grulla and Windy's dun mare among the several other horses and then moved quietly, speaking softly, patting a nervous flank here, a neck there. The animals moved restlessly, then quieted.

He untied the dun mare and Jim's grulla and led them away from the others. Saddles were arranged along the wall by the door. He found those he wanted and saddled the two horses, noting that Long Jim's Sharps and Windy's Winchester were still in their saddle scabbards, and their holster belts and guns were draped around the saddlehorn.

He did not pause to mentally question this oversight by men desperately in need of weapons and ammunition, although it was possible El Porcito had seen no urgency in distributing these weapons belonging to men due to be executed in the morning.

Quietly he led the animals out of the stable, then pulled back, freezing, as one of the men sleeping inside the old barracks came out and urinated against the wall. He yawned sleepily and went back inside.

Quickly then Felipe led the horses through a break in the presidio wall and back to where he had tied Betsy. The camel eyed these intruders with suspicious stare, but Felipe picketed the two horses far enough away to avoid possible disagreement.

He went back to the wall and slipped across the parade ground, pausing by the carreta. Celestino was snoring softly, the muzzle loader scrunched against his side.

Felipe tried to ease the rifle from him. The old man stiffened slightly and began mumbling something in Mexican. Felipe pulled back.

The man began to rub his eyes. Felipe slipped away. He should not have tried to take the rifle, he thought. Now he'd have to try something else.

Then a smile licked across his face as his hand slipped inside his pocket. He circled back to the stable and slipped inside. He found hay in a corner and made a small pile of it, away from the horses. Then he took out his small hoard of firecrackers and carefully dispersed them in the hay pile.

He hesitated, eyeing the horses . . . then went to them, carefully loosening their picket ropes so that a quick jerk would free them. He waited a moment, his gaze roving to the lantern casting a dim glow at the far end of the stable.

The boy smiled. He picked up some straw and held it over the lamp chimney, and when it caught fire he ran with it to the hay pile he had made. He waited just long enough to see the flames begin to lick up from the hay, then made a quick exit.

Celestino turned. He was standing beside the carreta, scratching himself, when he heard the horses neigh. He grabbed his rifle and waited, swiveling a startled gaze toward the stable. A small glow appeared inside . . . then one of the horses broke loose and dashed outside, onto the parade ground.

Celestino muttered a surprised curse. He started to run toward the stable, then suddenly stopped as a sharp report sounded inside. He kneeled and fired wildly into the barn and then as the firecrackers began to go off, sounding like rifle fire, he backed off, yelling.

Long Jim and Windy jerked awake. Windy snarled: 'What in tarnation—?'

A shadow slipped up behind them, holding a knife. Long Jim twisted aside, snarling, then went still as he saw Felipe kneel beside him.

Across the parade ground El Porcito burst out of the headquarters building, barefoot, his pants sliding dawn around his hips, a Colt in his hand. He paused, turning, as four cursing men came running out of the barracks.

Celestino pointed. 'In there, El Generale . . . we are being attacked!'

A report from inside the stable sent him scurrying into the shadows. El Porcito stood his ground, firing into the stable. A couple of the others joined him.

All of the horses had broken loose now and were running madly around the parade ground. No one saw the three who slipped like shadows through a break in the old fort's wall. The firing and the yelling went on. The milling horses, smelling smoke and fire, broke out of the yard and scattered through the brush downslope.

Felipe led Windy and Long Jim to their picketed horses. Windy buckled his cartridge belt around his lean waist.

'What's going on—a raid?'

Felipe held up one of his last two firecrackers. Windy shook his head. 'Sounded like a blasted troop of Federales.'

They mounted and followed Felipe, mounted on Betsy, as he headed north toward the border.

Behind them the firing grew louder . . . and finally faded.

CHAPTER NINE

The stars paled. A wind blew steadily from the north, bringing patches of cloud across the lightening sky. Slowly the shadowy hills began to emerge from the night.

Windy and Long Jim pulled up before the cabin where Farrow and Bill Sawyer had made their field headquarters. The boy watched from the back of the camel.

'You still want to find Mister Farrow?'

Windy nodded. 'That's what we came for.' And added under his breath, a grim look in his eyes. 'If he's still alive.'

The cabin stood still and silent, keeping its secrets. Long Jim swung tiredly down from his saddle.

'I don't know about you,' the stringbean said to Windy, 'but I'm gonna get something to eat, then grab a little shut-eye.'

Windy grunted.

'Come on, kid,' he said. 'We'll camp here.'

He looked off toward the south. 'Don't reckon El Porcito will come after us, do you?'

The boy grinned. 'Not tonight, señor. Tomorrow . . . ?' He shrugged. 'Quien sabe?'

He touched the camel's neck and the ungainly beast went down on folded knees. Felipe slipped down from between the humps.

Long Jim eyed him suspiciously. 'Where'd a

squirt like you learn to ride that thing?'

'Mister Farrow,' the boy said proudly. 'He teach me a lot of things.'

'Like stealing an' lying?' Long Jim turned to his grizzled partner. 'What kind of jasper is yore nephew?'

'No, no . . . not steal.' The boy's voice held a wistful note. 'Mister Farrow is great man. He teach me to read. He tell me about Mexico . . . about my people. He make me feel good—'

'Didn't yuh go to school?'

'School?' Felipe backed off, eyeing them warily.

Windy growled. 'Where're yore folks?'

Felipe looked puzzled.

'Yore ma and pa!' Windy snapped. 'Everybody has em.'

The boy looked sad. 'I don't remember them, señor. Only my sister. And Ramon. And they always fight—'

'Sounds natural,' Long Jim said.

Windy scratched his nose. 'What did Quincy do out here besides teaching yuh what yuh oughta know anyway?'

'Look for rocks,' the boy replied. 'He and Mister Sawyer put them in boxes. Once a week they ride to Goliath and ship them somewhere.'

'That all they did?'

The boy pointed toward a distant silhouette against the sky. 'Sometimes Mister Farrow ride to that montana. He take his spyglass with him

68

and he spend much time there.'

'You know what he was looking for?'

The boy hesitated. 'Guns, I think, señor.'

Windy glanced at his partner, frowning. 'Guns?' He turned back to the boy.

'Guns for who?'

The boy shook his head, but his eyes were evasive. Windy grabbed him by his oversize shirt and pulled him close.

'For El Porcito?'

'Maybe,' the boy said. 'I . . . I heard Ramon talk tonight . . . he tell my sister El Porcito received word. The guns are ready.'

Windy let the boy go. He studied the long flat mountain against the horizon, remembering the circle he had seen on the wall map in El Porcito's office.

He pointed. 'That is El Rojo?'

Felipe nodded.

Windy scratched in his dusty beard stubble. Long Jim frowned. 'Looks like something's going on we shouldn't know about,' he said. 'And yore nephew is neck-deep in trouble.'

They picketed the animals and Long Jim and the boy ate hungrily from cans of beans, peaches and hominy. It was a strange combination, but there was not much choice in the cabin.

Windy ate sparingly and went outside, thumbing tobacco into his old corncob from an oilskin pouch. He eyed the distant hill. If Quincy were still alive, he was probably being

69

held captive somewhere in that area. By whom? El Porcito had denied knowing what had happened to Farrow, and Windy was inclined to believe him.

The morning birds began to chirp in the brush. Windy knocked the remains of his tobacco from his pipe and ground them under his heel. He was tired. It had been a long, long day.

They turned in and fell instantly asleep. The sun rose above the barren hills and sent its warming rays down the sides of the jagged hills.

Windy was still sleeping when Long Jim shook him.

'The boy's gone,' he said.

Windy slipped on his boots and went outside. It was already warm. He scratched his head.

'Didn't figger he'd still be here,' he confessed.

'Think he went back to San Juan?'

'With El Porcito waiting to shoot him?' Windy grinned. 'He's wary as a coyote, an' about as hard to catch. I figger he's gone looking for Quincy.'

Long Jim glanced toward the jagged hills. 'We could spend a week chousin' among them hills an' not find anything.'

'Don't intend to,' Windy growled. 'We're going back to Goliath.'

'Goliath!' Long Jim snorted. 'Why, yuh

blankety-blank pinhead, after what you did to thet depitty we'll be about as welcome there as a rattler in an old ladies' prayer meeting!'

Windy shrugged. 'I'll apologize,' he said. There was a twinkle in his blue eyes. 'Hell, a bump on the head ain't nothing to get all fired up over.'

He walked past Jim to his horse and started to saddle the mare.

' 'Sides,' he said calmly, and there was a grimness in his voice now, 'I want to check on that missing suitcase of my nephew's.'

Long Jim sighed. 'Hope that deppity is an understanding man,' he said. He saddled his grulla and checked the loads in his Frontier.

'Be jest about time to eat again, by time we reach town,' he said.

Windy grunted. 'Some day yo're gonna eat something that's gonna give yuh a howling case of indigestion.'

'What's that?' Long Jim asked innocently.

'Oh, cripes!' Windy growled, and swung his cayuse toward Goliath.

*   *   *

Jip Jenkins walked into the newspaper office and stood watching the flat-bed press banging away. Paul Incalis was talking to the operator, a thin-faced, sallow man with a stub of cigar in his mouth.

The *Border Inquirer* was a four-page weekly,

71

but its fiery editorials and free-swinging news style had earned it a wide circulation throughout the Territory. Because of it Paul Incalis wielded considerable influence, especially among the border towns.

He said, 'I want a thousand copies ready to go out on the night stage, Lou. We'll get the others ready for the morning run to Lewisburg.'

The operator nodded. 'I'll need help for the morning editor—'

'Hire who you need,' Paul said. He saw Jenkins waiting for him by the slug boxes and walked to him.

The deputy said, 'Got to see yuh, Paul,' and the newspaper publisher frowned at this familiarity. He nodded curtly toward his office.

They went inside and Paul closed the door, dimming the clatter of the press in the shop. It was little more than a cubbyhole, this office, with a window fronting on the street.

'Where's the sheriff?' Jip growled.

'Gone to Palmer.' Paul sat behind his cluttered desk and plucked a cigar from his private box. 'Damn fool had stomach trouble again. He's given up on Doc Browder and went to see a breed woman with mystic healing powers.'

'Christ!' Jensen growled. 'If only he'd quit eating like a hog—'

'We don't need him, anyway,' Paul said.

'When's the shipment due?'

Paul glanced at the clock. 'Inside an hour . . . if it's on time.' He got up and walked to the window. 'I'm taking it out myself, this time.'

Jensen looked surprised.

'I'll leave early, before most folks are up. If anyone asks, I've gone to Palmer, too.'

Jensen frowned. 'El Porcito take the bait?'

Paul Incalis smiled. 'He can't afford not to.' He looked out into the street. 'If things go right, he should be hitting Goliath by sundown tomorrow. You ready?'

'They won't have a chance,' Jensen said. He walked to the desk and appropriated a cigar. 'Some things worry me, Paul. Sawyer being killed—'

'By that Mexican bandit, El Porcito,' the newspaper man said. He chuckled coldly. 'Read all about it in the *Border Inquirer*.'

'Folks hereabouts will believe it,' Jensen said. 'But what if the governor sends down an investigator? Or the cavalry?'

'Seventh Cavalry's tied up with that Apache trouble up north,' Incalis said. 'And why should anyone want an investigation?'

'Mebbe yo're right, Paul,' Jensen said, relaxing. He lighted up, breathed deeply. 'But those two old saddle bums who rode into town the other day . . . one of them claimin' to be kin of Farrow—'

'Probably long gone,' Incalis said complacently. 'Anyway, they won't bother us again.'

'Just the same,' the deputy growled, 'I'd like to see that pint-sized bum once more—'

He headed for the door, suddenly wheeled around and went back to the window.

'Paul!'

The newspaperman's eyes narrowed. 'Let them be, Jip!'

Jensen shook his head. 'I got a score to settle.' His hand dropped down to his gun. 'This time I'm gonna hold the winning hand!'

CHAPTER TEN

Windy eased his dun mare aside as Jensen stepped into the street ahead of them. Long Jim leaned indolently over his saddlehorn and eyed the gun in the deputy's hand.

'No need of that, deppity,' he said. 'We came to give ourselfs up. An' I want to apologize for my partner, Windy.'

Jensen shifted his muzzle toward the pint-sized oldster. 'Reckon you figgered you could play fast an' loose with the law in this town an' get away with it, eh? Well, yuh got another think coming, pop!'

'Yuh got me wrong,' Windy said. 'Didn't mean anything—'

'Where's the boy?'

'Boy?' Windy stared blankly for a moment, then: 'Oh, that thieving varmint!' He shook his head, his voice going mournful. 'Promised he'd lead me to my nephew. Then stole us blind.' He reached into a pants pocket and turned it inside out. 'Lucky for us he left us our cayuses.'

'I'm bustin' a gut cryin',' Jensen sneered.

Long Jim looked angry. 'That's a hell of a way to look at it, deppity. You should be out chasin' after that thief 'stead of threatening innocent citizens.'

'Get down!' Jensen snarled rudely. 'An'

75

keep yore hands high!'

Long Jim sighed as he looked at Windy. The pint-sized oldster's blue eyes snapped angrily. 'Told yuh we shouldn't'a' come back!'

He slipped out of saddle under Jensen's threatening muzzle and held his hands shoulder-high.

'Where's the sheriff?' he said, glancing toward the law office up the street. 'I want to lodge a complaint.'

'The sheriff's out of town!' Jensen snapped. 'I reckon a spell in the calaboose will cool yuh both off.'

A coldness crept into Windy's gaze. 'Seems to me yo're carrying this a little too far, deppity. I apologized. I figger that's enough. Besides, my partner didn't have anything to do with what happened to you.'

'Don't matter,' Jensen snarled. 'I'm jailing both of you, just to teach you a lessen!'

A sizeable group of onlookers had come out to the walks to watch. It was unexpected excitement in what had been a dull afternoon.

Windy glanced at his partner and the tall man recognized the look in the grizzled man's eyes. He grinned faintly and edged away from his mount.

'I ain't going to no jail!' Windy said flatly. He pointed to the gun in Jensen's hand. 'You want to use that thing, you go right ahead an' shoot!'

He turned his back on the surprised lawman

76

and started leading his cayuse toward the Tolbert House.

Jip Jensen rocked on his toes, his eyes narrowing. 'Yuh old fool.' He was aware of the spectators watching the old man defy him and he took a step forward, cocking his Colt. 'One more step—'

Long Jim said sharply, 'You shoot him and yo're a dead man, deppity!'

Jensen stiffened. He had momentarily forgotten Long Jim and now he saw that the tall man was standing to one side, his gunhand down by his side.

Jensen's gunhand trembled and an ugly look came into his eyes. He was caught in a Mexican standoff, but he hated to swallow his pride and back down. For a long dragging moment death balanced on a razor's edge in that hot and dusty street.

Then Paul Incalis stepped out of the newspaper office and took Jensen off the hook.

'No call to kill anyone, Jip,' he said, coming down the stairs toward them. 'Let them be.'

Jensen licked his lips, eased his hammer down and in a sudden angry movement jammed the gun back into its holster.

Windy turned to the newspaperman. 'Much obliged,' he said.

Paul said, 'I heard you had left town?'

Windy nodded. 'Went looking for my nephew. You know, Quincy Farrow.'

'Oh?' Paul made a surprised gesture. 'Too bad you didn't get back sooner. You just missed him.'

Windy looked surprised. 'He was in Goliath?'

'Came and went,' Paul said. 'Left on last night's stage. But he left a note for you.' He pointed toward the Tolbert House. 'I told him you'd been by.'

Windy's face was still for a moment, revealing nothing. Then he shook his head. 'Wal, I'll be damned,' he said, looking at Long Jim. 'Goes to show, yuh can't trust any of these youngsters today.'

He turned back to the newspaper man. 'He say where he was going?'

'Was in too much of a hurry, I guess. I told him about his partner, Sawyer, and he said he'd stand the funeral expenses.' Paul shrugged. 'Guess he ran into trouble out there with some of El Porcito's boys. Anyway, he's gone.

Windy scratched his beard. 'Mebbe he left word with the hotel clerk?'

'Could be,' Paul said.

They went inside the Tolbert House, leaving their mounts tied to the rack. The clerk was standing stiffly behind the counter; he seemed to be expecting them.

'I told them about Mister Farrow,' Paul said.

A nervous smile twitched across the clerk's face. 'Oh, yes.' He reached behind and took a folded piece of notepaper from a pigeonhole. He handed it to Windy.

'Mr. Farrow left this for you, Mister Harris.'

Windy read the message aloud. '"Paul Incalis told me you were in town, looking for me. Sorry to have missed you. Give my love to ma.'

It was signed, in an almost illegible scrawl, 'Quincy Farrow.'

Windy scratched his head. 'He just up an' left, eh? Didn't even say where?'

The clerk licked his lips. 'Not a word. Just packed up and left.'

Windy turned to his partner. 'Wal, reckon there's no accounting for bad manners,' he grumbled. 'Haven't seen the boy in near twenty years, an' he doesn't even bother to hang around a day or two—'

Paul asked politely, 'You'll be leaving Goliath?'

'Not right away,' Windy said. He turned to the clerk. 'Mind if we use my nephew's room?' He turned to Paul. 'We're plumb tuckered out. Here we were, wandering around out there looking for the damn fool an' Quincy was here in town all the while.'

The clerk glanced at the newspaper man and Paul nodded imperceptibly.

'Hope the deppity doesn't mind,' Windy said innocently. 'We'll be leaving in the morning.'

Paul shrugged. 'I'll talk to him,' he

promised. He took some money out of his pocket and placed it on the counter. 'Room's on me,' he said.

Windy started to protest.

'Heard you tell Jensen that Mex boy stole everything you had,' Paul said.

'That's right,' Long Jim said quickly.

Windy sighed. 'Plumb forgot.' He nodded to Paul. 'Thanks.'

'Hospitality of the town,' Paul said. He walked to the door and paused.

'You didn't happen to run into any of El Porcito's bandits out there, did you?'

'Only thing we ran into was sand and rocks,' Windy grumbled. 'The boy brought us to a shack out in the middle of nowhere and said it was Quincy's camp. Then, when we was sleeping, he lit out. Tried to take our cayuses, but they got away from him, I reckon. Took us most of the day to round them up.'

He looked down at his feet and sighed. 'Reckon I'm getting too old for this sort of thing.'

Paul grinned. 'Time does catch up on a man,' he said. He waved shortly. 'Hope you run into your nephew somewhere along the line.'

'Not if I can help it,' Windy said, disgruntled. He waited until Paul had gone, then he looked at his partner.

'Wal, what are yuh waiting for?' he demanded peevishly.

The clerk watched them go up the stairs, arguing about smart-alecky nephews and thieving Mexicans, but he was not reassured.

CHAPTER ELEVEN

Quincy Farrow's room was still hot from the day's heat. If Quincy had come back, Windy thought, he had not stayed long enough to air it out. But the room did look as though his nephew had hastily vacated it. His old bathrobe still hung on a hook in the closet. Some socks lay at the foot of the bed, and old slippers peeked out from under the washstand.

Long Jim said, 'Whew!' and went to open the window. Windy settled on the bed and shook his head.

'Ain't like the boy to leave like that,' he said. 'I know his ma. She brung him up right, even if she did fuss too much over him when he was a button.'

Long Jim eyed the flat roof just below the window. The sun was going down but heat waves still shimmered the surface.

'You figger somebody's lying?'

Windy shrugged.

'That note he left,' Long Jim growled, coming back toward his partner. 'That yore nephew's writing?'

'How in hell would I know?' Windy snapped irritably. 'I told yuh I ain't seen the boy since he was a pup.

Long Jim wandered around the room. 'Not much we can do here now. If yore nephew's gone—'

'I ain't sure he ever came to town,' Windy growled. He tossed his hat on the bed and riffled his fingers through thinning hair. 'He and Sawyer were up to something, Jim. They even went to see El Porcito. Then Sawyer was shot. And Quincy disappears—until today. He comes in and goes right out, kinda convenient like.'

He got up and walked to the window and looked out toward the distant hills.

'Anybody could have written that note, Jim.'

'That pimply-faced clerk?'

'Or that newspaper man, Paul Incalis,' Windy growled. He walked back and picked up his hat. 'Let's go find out.'

Long Jim knuckled his jaw. 'What about that deppity?'

Windy eyed him with level gaze. 'We won't hurt him—unless he gets in the way.'

They went downstairs and crossed the lobby to the desk. An older man, deep furrows in a dissipated face, eyed them questioningly.

'Where is he?' Windy snapped. 'The pimply-faced feller who runs this shebang?'

'Snopes?' The desk man gave Windy a wry smile. 'Gone home for supper. And he doesn't run this hotel, he just works here. I'm the relief man.'

Long Jim said, 'Who owns this place then?'

'Mister Incalis.'

'The newspaper man?'

The desk clerk nodded. 'Owns half of Goliath.'

Windy eyed him. 'He own you?'

The clerk stiffened slightly. 'Nobody owns me.'

'That other clerk, Snopes, said Quincy Farrow was in here yesterday. You see him?'

The clerk's eyes shadowed. 'No. But he could have been.'

Windy drew his Colt and laid it on the counter, his palm resting lightly on it.

'We're looking for a missing suitcase,' he said gently. 'Farrow's. You seen it?'

The clerk's eyes narrowed and he wet his lips.

'Are you threatening me?'

'Persuading is the word,' Windy said.

The man shook his head. 'Snopes checked Farrow and Sawyer in and he was the one who checked Farrow out. I just work relief here.'

Windy slipped his Colt back into his holster and eyed the desk clerk with faint admiration. The man had not been frightened at all.

'What do you do beside riding this desk job?'

'Gamble a little.' The man suddenly looked uncomfortable.

'Bet you handle a gun pretty well, too,' Windy said.

A guarded look came into the man's eyes. 'Not me,' he said coldly. 'Don't like the noise.'

Windy snorted. 'I'll bet.'

They went outside and stood on the hotel steps, eyeing the town. There was not much activity on Goliath's street, but then there never was.

A shirt-sleeved man wearing a green eyeshade came out of a small building down the street and looked toward the desert road. The sign over the doorway read: GREAT WESTERN STAGELINES.

He waited for a moment, then went back inside.

Windy said, 'I got an idea—'

'Save it,' Long Jim growled. He was eyeing the lunchroom across the street. 'Let's eat first.'

They were about to cross the street when a wagon came around the corner and headed toward them. The driver was a heavily bearded, stocky man, dust-caked from a long ride. A canvas was lashed tight over his cargo. A cold-eyed man with a rifle across his knees was riding shotgun.

The wagon rolled past them. Paul Incalis came out of his office and waited until the wagon turned into the *Border Inquirer*'s yard and headed for the shed in back, then he followed it.

'Mighty important cargo,' Long Jim mused.

Windy nudged his partner. Jensen had stepped out of the Red Bucket saloon as the wagon rolled by. He gave them a look and then walked quickly toward the newspaper office.

'Thick as thieves,' Windy muttered. 'Wonder what's in that wagon that's so important?'

'Newsprint,' Long Jim said innocently.

The man in the green eyeshade came out of the stage office again and looked east. The shadows were beginning to shroud the desert hills, turning them purple. A cool breeze sprang up and chased bits of paper and sand down the street.

Windy grabbed his partner's arm. 'We'll eat later,' he growled.

The stage station manager went inside before they reached him. He was behind a cluttered desk, muttering over bills when they entered.

'The stage's late,' the man said crossly, 'you'll have to wait.' He waved toward a corner of the room. 'Put your bags over there.'

Then he raised his eyes and saw the two oldsters and frowned. 'Thought you were the passengers who bought tickets this afternoon.' He got up and went to a small rolltop desk. 'How far you going?'

'Which way is the stage headed?'

The station man turned his head, frowning. 'Stage's due in from Palmer, east of here. It'll be going west . . . first stop Lordsville, then Albuquerque, connecting with—'

'That's far enough,' Windy interrupted. 'We ain't going anywhere.'

The man shoved a bundle of tickets back into a pigeonhole. He ran his eyes over them more closely now, seeing two dusty, unshaven men with enough gray in their hair to mislead him.

'Look,' he said crossly, 'I'm busy. The saloon's across the street—'

'We ben thinkin' about it,' Windy said. 'Right now we got something else on our minds.'

He paused and turned to the door as a man wheeling a pushcart stopped just outside. He picked up a bundle of papers and came inside and dropped it by the door, then went back for another. He set this one down beside the other, glanced at Windy and Long Jim and tossed a rolled-up issue of the *Border Inquirer* on the desk.

'Mr. Incalis wants you to make sure this gets loaded on the stage, Mr. Sloane.'

Everett Sloane nodded. 'If it gets here,' he muttered. He glanced at his pocket watch. 'It's an hour late already.'

The man from the *Border Inquirer* shrugged and left. Sloane turned to the two oldsters.

'What is it?' His tone was sharp.

'We want to know if Quincy Farrow left on last night's stage?'

'Farrow?' Sloane's brow furrowed. 'Oh, you mean that geologist fellow from back East. He was staying at the Tolbert House.'

'That's him.'

'Don't remember seeing him. Fact is, don't recall seeing him in town much, either.'

'Anyone else besides you work here?'

Sloane shook his head. 'Couple of baggage handlers I hire by the day. Why?'

'I'm Farrow's uncle,' Windy said. 'Came to town to look him up. They told me he left on the stage last night.'

'Who told you?'

'Paul Incalis.'

A small shock went through the station manager. He turned quickly and fumbled through some papers. 'If Paul said he left, then he did.' His voice sounded strained.

'But you didn't see Farrow get on that stage?'

Sloane slowly turned to them. His manner was cold now, brusque.

'No. But that doesn't mean he couldn't have boarded it.'

Long Jim walked to the desk. 'Don't you keep a passenger list?'

Sloane said tightly, 'Not always.' He pulled out his pocket watch again, a nervous gesture. 'Look, I've got my own troubles—'

Shots rang out on the still air. A volley of them on the far end of town, coming closer. A faint whooping came with it . . . then more shots. And the sound of wheels churning desert sand . . .

Sloane said, 'The stage!' and pushed past Windy on his way out.

CHAPTER TWELVE

The stage slewed into sight around a bend in the road, raising a cloud of dust. It brought most of Goliath's citizens out to watch, for the arrival of the stage was the only event to break the day's torpor.

The stage careened madly down the street, frightening dogs and children, leaving a banner of dust in its wake. The driver, a redheaded runt of a man with gnarled hands and an impish sense of humor, fired his last shot into the air before thrusting the rifle back into its saddle boot and swinging the four-horse team around to a stop in front of Sloane, standing in front of the stage office door.

'What in the devil do you think you're doing?' Sloane said wrathfully. 'Goddammit, Tad, I warned you—'

'Bandits!' Tad cut him off. 'Must have been about a hundred of them.' But he was grinning and Sloane knew he was lying.

Tad swung down and opened the stage door. 'Thirty minute stop, folks. Jest time to wash up an' eat.' He stepped back, grinning expectantly.

A couple of ashen-faced men emerged, drummers from their looks. They seemed glad to be on solid ground.

'Hotel's that way,' Tad said cheerfully.

'Saloon's across the street.'

The two passengers staggered away.

Sloane said grimly, 'Tad, I want to see you inside.'

He paused, staring as the last passenger emerged from the dusty coach. She was a tall, beautiful redhead, middle twenties, fair-skinned with a faint spattering of freckles across her nose. She clung for a moment to the side of the stage door, a crushed, flowered hat tilted over one snapping green eye.

'We're here, ma'am,' Tad said, grinning. 'This is Goliath.'

She gave him a withering look as she pushed her hat back from her forehead.

'I didn't see any bandits.'

'We outran 'em,' Tad said, unabashed.

She turned her gaze to Sloane standing nearby. 'Are you in charge here?'

Sloane nodded uncomfortably. 'I'm sorry, ma'am—'

She cut him off. 'I want to send a wire to Washington! To President Hayes . . . he's a family friend.' She stepped down, glared at Tad. 'This man has no regard for the life or limb of his passengers. A tobacco-chewing, irresponsible barbarian, he . . . he belongs in a cage.'

Tad said, as though it were a compliment, 'Yes, ma'am.' He climbed up to the baggage section and threw several bags down on the ground. 'Yore luggage, ma'am.'

Sloane said weakly, 'I'm sure your complaints are well-founded. But the nearest telegraph office is sixty miles away—'

She fixed him with an icy stare.

'But I'll see that your complaints get to the main office,' he said hastily.

She glanced toward the stage office doorway where Windy and Long Jim were watching. She crooked a finger at them.

'Come here, my good man!'

Windy looked at Long Jim. His partner frowned. 'Means you, I reckon.'

'You!' the girl said imperiously, pointing to Long Jim. 'Take my bags to the hotel!'

Long Jim said, 'Hold on, ma'am. I ain't—'

But she had turned away from them, to Sloane. 'I want that driver fired. Immediately.' Her voice held a cold anger. 'Tobacco chewing and whiskey drinking, on a public conveyance! I'll see that my husband hears of this!'

She swung back to Long Jim. 'What are you waiting for?'

Windy nudged his partner; he was grinning widely. 'Yuh heard the lady, Jim. Get her bags!'

Jim tucked a small carpetbag under his left arm and picked up the other two bags. They were heavy. He gave Windy a dirty look as he followed the girl toward the hotel.

'Real lady,' Windy said admiringly. 'Knows her own mind, too.' He looked at Sloane. 'Who is she?'

91

Sloane glanced at the driver. Tad scratched his head. 'Said her name was Farrow . . . Linda Farrow.'

Windy whirled. The girl and Long Jim were disappearing inside the hotel.

'Know her?' Sloane asked. He was still sweating.

'Not yet,' Windy said grimly. 'But I will.'

* * *

Ritchie Snopes had come hack from supper in time to be confronted by the green-eyed, redheaded girl in crumpled hat and dust-caked traveling clothes. He had returned cowed and sullen from a session with his waspish wife and his meal lay heavy on his stomach. He was not prepared for the girl who faced him across the counter. His gaze wandered to Long Jim who dropped the bags on the floor a few feet behind her.

'My room, please. And I want my bath drawn immediately!'

'Your room?' Snopes looked sullen. 'I'm sorry but I don't believe I have a reservation—'

'Mrs. Linda Farrow!' the girl said impatiently. 'My husband made the reservation more than a week ago!'

Snopes blanched. 'Mrs. Farrow—'

Long Jim straightened, then turned as Windy came inside the hotel. Windy brushed past him on his way to the desk.

Linda Farrow was shaking a finger at Snopes. 'Don't just stand there, boy! Show me to my room!'

Windy said, 'Mrs. Farrow!' and she turned, annoyed.

'Yes?'

'Are you kin to Quincy Farrow?'

She looked him over as though inspecting an insect. 'You know my husband?'

'Only when he was a boy,' Windy said. 'I'm his uncle.'

She shuddered. 'I don't believe it.'

'Wal, yuh better believe it, ma'am,' Windy growled. He eyed her, a bit awed. 'I don't remember my sister writing me Quincy was married.'

Linda Farrow gave him a cold stare. 'My good man,' she said haughtily, 'I don't know who you are. But you can't be related to my husband.' She ran her gaze over his dusty, disreputable appearance again and shuddered. 'Not the Farrows of Quincy, Mass!'

She turned back to Snopes. 'Is my husband in?'

Snopes shook his head, his mouth open.

'Tell him I want to see him when he returns.' She made a commanding gesture with her hand. 'Now—my room, please!'

Snopes groped for a key behind him and went around the counter. Linda turned to Long Jim. 'Bring my bags, boy. You,' she said sharply to Windy, 'give him a hand!'

93

She swept away after Snopes before either of them could speak.

Long Jim was awed. 'Yore nephew's wife! No wonder he left town!'

He picked up a bag and handed it to Windy. 'Come on, boy!' he grinned. 'Before she gets real mad!'

They followed the girl and Snopes upstairs. Snopes opened the room across the hall from theirs. He went inside, the girl following.

She blanched at the stored heat. 'My God!' she gasped. 'Don't you ever air this place out?'

The clerk hurriedly opened the window. The curtain flapped slightly as a breeze came in.

Linda dropped her hat on the bed. 'My bath,' she reminded Snopes.

'Yes, ma'am,' he said and scurried for the door, bumping into Long Jim and Windy coining in.

'And—' Snopes paused and looked back to her. 'I'll have breakfast served in my room at eight-thirty sharp! Coffee, crumpets and a dab of honey. You get that, boy?'

Snopes nodded and left the room.

She watched Long Jim and Windy drop her bags by the bed. A faint pity came into her eyes.

'Here,' she said, pressing a silver dollar into Windy's palm. 'For both of you.'

Windy eyed the coin. 'Ma'am—' he started to say, but she pushed him toward the door. 'I know it's more than you expected. But you do seem to need it.' She turned to Long Jim, her voice becoming severe. 'See that he doesn't spend it all on whiskey!'

She closed the door behind them and they heard the key turn in the lock.

Windy had a dazed look in his eyes as Long Jim led him away.

CHAPTER THIRTEEN

Snopes was nowhere in sight when they went back down into the lobby.

'Getting her bath, probably,' Windy muttered and looked back toward the stairs.

Long Jim pulled him away. 'We'll talk to him later. Right now we're gonna eat.'

They crossed the street to the lunchroom they had spotted earlier. It was run by a former Southern Pacific railroad worker named Won Chang who had shed his queue, married a Mexican girl and decided to stay in Goliath.

They had egg foo yang and chili con carne, which turned out to be a strangely satisfying combination. Long Jim had two helpings.

It was getting dark when they stepped outside. The stage was getting ready to leave. Two well-fortified drummers emerged from the saloon and crossed on unsteady feet to the stagecoach. Tad poured them into the carriage and left Goliath the way he had arrived—in a cloud of dust and a volley of rifle shots.

'Sure gets a kick outa his job,' Windy observed.

They started back for the hotel to see if Quincy's green-eyed wife had finished with her bath, but got side-tracked by the barbershop.

Windy ran his fingers through his gritty beard. 'Ain't had a shave in a week,' he remembered. He eyed his partner. 'How long since you had a bath?'

'Last time we crossed the Rio Grande!' Long Jim snapped. 'That was the time you near drowned, you idjit!'

Windy was unabashed by this. 'Could stand another.' He was thinking of the way Quincy's wife had looked at him. 'Hell, won't hurt us none.'

They went inside.

The two chairs were empty. A door to a back room had a sign that read: BATHS— TWO BITS.

The barber, a one-eyed man with thick, hairy arms and a saucer-wide baldspot on his head was reading the *Border Inquirer.*

'That's right, dammit!' he was muttering. 'Give 'em hell—'

He looked up as the two oldsters entered. 'Shave?'

Windy nodded. 'Haircut an' bath, too.' He settled himself in one of the two empty chairs. 'Don't spare the lather. I got a tender skin.'

The barber stuck his head into the back room and yelled, 'Steve—customers!' and a younger man with a lazy slouch and a sour expression emerged. He waved Long Jim to the other chair and tucked an apron under his chin.

'The works,' Jim said.

Steve surveyed the tangled, gritty beard and shook his head. 'Oughta charge yuh double, pop.' He began to strop his razor.

The barber thrust the newspaper under Windy's nose. 'What do you think about it, mister? That damn Mex bandit, El Porcito, is threatening to raid us.'

Windy shrugged. 'Be a fool to try it, I say.'

But the barber was worried. 'Paper says he's got over a hundred well-armed men. Christ! That's enough to wipe out half a dozen border towns.'

Windy glanced at Long Jim, whose face was hidden beneath a mass of lather. He was trying to jibe the half-dozen poorly armed men he had seen in El Porcito's camp with Paul Incalis's fiery editorial.

'Damn chuckle-headed politicians up in Santa Fe keep sitting on their hands,' the barber continued, brushing lather into Windy's whiskers. They're worried about Geronimo, but I say to hell with them. The Seventh Cavalry should be down here right now—'

He continued grumbling throughout the process of shaving Windy and cutting his hair. Both oldsters were glad to escape into the back room where they luxuriated in large wooden tubs and lukewarm water.

They emerged an hour later, cleaner and refreshed in spirit, but still worried about Quincy Farrow and concerned over the woman who said she was his wife.

Long Jim ran his palm across his smooth-shaven cheek. 'Feel kinda unprotected,' he muttered and eyed his partner in the light from the barbershop.

The face that had emerged from the grayshot, wiry beard was thin, strong and faintly humorous. The skin was clear and brown and except for the spiderweb lines around the hard blue eyes remarkably unwrinkled.

Both men seemed to have shed ten years.

Long Jim sniffed. 'Smell like a rose,' he commented. 'Think she'll recognize us?'

Windy shrugged. His gaze was on the lighted window of the *Border Inquirer*.

'I ben thinking,' he said, 'about El Porcito.'

Long Jim snorted. 'El Generale?'

'That newspaperman's got the town all stirred up.'

'Over nothing,' Long Jim growled. 'Cripes, Windy—we both know El Porcito ain't got enough guns and men to break up a Sunday school picnic.'

'What if he got the guns he needed?'

Long Jim frowned, mulling this over.

'I'd like to take a look at what was in that wagon,' Windy said.

Long Jim turned his gaze toward the *Border Inquirer*. 'Sure,' he grinned, 'let's walk over an' ask Mr. Incalis—'

He paused as a figure came out of the saloon a few buildings down and turned toward them. Both men waited until Deputy Jensen strode up.

Windy said, 'Evenin', deppity.'

Jensen whirled, his hand on his gun. He eyed the two oldsters, not recognizing them.

Long Jim said casually, 'Bygones be bygones, fella?'

Jensen settled back on his heels. 'Yuh smell a little better,' he sneered, 'but a shave an' bath don't change the stripes of a polecat.'

Long Jim stiffened, but Windy said meekly, 'We ain't looking for no trouble, deppity.'

Jensen's voice hardened. 'I want both you saddle bums off the street an' outa town by sunup. Now get moving!'

Windy pulled at Long Jim's arm and they went across the street to the hotel.

Snopes was behind the counter when they entered. He looked harassed.

'Mrs. Farrow still in her room?'

He nodded. 'Still soaking, by God!' He mopped his brow. 'Maid's been up there five times.'

'You tell her her husband left town?'

'Me?' Snopes stared at Windy. 'Hell, I can't even get a word in edgewise!'

Windy shrugged. 'We're turning in. Call us before the stage leaves in the morning?'

Snopes nodded and they went upstairs. Windy paused to knock on Linda's door. There was the sound of splashing, then a cold voice said, 'Go away!'

Windy glanced at Long Jim. His partner shrugged.

They went into their room, which had cooled off somewhat. Long Jim lighted the lamp. Windy went to the window and looked out. The flat roof was just below him.

'I'm still thinking of that wagon,' he said.

They slipped out through the window and crossed at a crouch to the back of the building. They hung from the roof for a moment, looking down into the blackness of the yard, then dropped.

A startled alley cat gave a *yeowl* and streaked off.

They were not far from the *Border Inquirer* building. The flatbed press was still banging away. Evidently this was to be a big edition.

They scaled a low board fence and came up behind the long open-faced shed that made the bottom leg of the L-shaped newspaper building.

They circled cautiously, staying inside the deep shadows. A loading platform ran alongside the shop and light from within cast a faint glow into the yard.

Long Jim nudged his partner and pointed.

A tall shadow moved across their line of vision, a rifle cradled in his right arm.

'They ain't taking no chances,' he breathed.

Windy nodded. He edged back slightly and his heel clinked softly against an empty bottle.

The guard stiffened, staring into the darkness.

Windy picked up the bottle. He whispered

something to Long Jim. His partner nodded, then slipped quietly away.

The guard said sharply, 'Who is it?'

He had his rifle ready now, peering into the shadows.

Windy tugged his battered hat down low over his eyes. He lurched forward, waving the empty bottle.

'That you, Harry?' His voice was thick, slurred.

The guard eased. 'Damn drunk!' He made a motion with the rifle.

'Get the hell outa here!'

Windy paused a few feet away. 'Hey! You ain't Harry.' He staggered a little as he looked around. 'Where's Harry?'

The guard took a step forward and didn't see Long Jim slip in behind him.

'I said get to hell outa here.'

Windy turned to go. He slipped and fell, dropping the bottle. The guard bent over him. 'A night in the calaboose will—'

He crumpled without a sound as Long Jim buffaloed him. Windy gave his partner a hand and they dragged the guard into the shed.

The wagon was backed up against the wall, its tarpaulin still lashed tight. It had not been unloaded.

A door opened onto the loading platform and two figures came out. Windy shot Long Jim a look. The stringbean picked up the guard's rifle, tugged his hat brim down over his eyes and moved out of the shed.

Paul Incalis was talking with his shop foreman. 'That oughta do it, Lou. Lock up and go to bed.'

The foreman went back inside and Paul turned to look toward the shed.

'Everything all right, Chris?'

Long Jim was a shadowy figure with a rifle across his arm. He waved and muttered something unintelligible.

Paul said, 'I'll have someone relieve you before midnight.'

Long Jim sighed softly as the newspaperman left. He turned and went back to join Windy, who had loosened a corner of the tarpaulin and was tugging at a long flat box. He helped Windy haul it clear and with the blade of a knife they pried the loosely nailed cover open.

Windy reached inside and pulled out a brand new Winchester repeating rifle.

Both men eyed it for a moment, thinking the same thoughts. Then Windy eased it back and replaced the cover and the tarp.

Long Jim said, 'They're gonna guess, Windy.'

The smaller man nodded. 'Let 'em. They can't prove it was us.'

Long Jim dropped the rifle beside the unconscious guard and they crossed back the way they had come. Long Jim boosted his grizzled partner up to the roof. Windy leaned over and gave him a hand and together they crossed to their hotel window.

They paused briefly inside to make sure no one had checked on them. Nothing seemed disturbed. They went out in the hall and listened by Linda's door. It was quiet inside. Windy knocked. No one answered.

They went down into the lobby.

Snopes was dozing behind his desk. He turned as Windy and Long Jim approached. He eyed them suspiciously.

Long Jim said mildly, 'Too tired to sleep.'

Windy said, 'Mrs. Farrow still soaking?'

Snopes sighed. 'She's in the dining room.'

Long Jim frowned. 'Didn't know you had one.'

Snopes pointed toward a door. 'Right through there.'

As Windy and Long Jim turned, 'You going to tell her about her husband?' His voice sounded hopeful.

'That's just what we intend to,' Windy growled.

They went inside the dining room, pausing by the cashier's desk . . . and became instantly aware that all eyes in the room, men and women, were on a diner eating alone at a corner table.

There was a regal, almost haughty quality about Linda Farrow as she daintily picked at her food with her fork. She had changed into a dress that was the latest in high fashion, to the envy of the women and the obvious admiration of the men.

Nothing like it had been seen in Goliath since Governor Wallace had made a tour with entourage some years back.

The elderly woman behind the cashier's cage picked up two menus and started for them, but Windy waved her away. He and Long Jim headed for Mrs. Farrow's table.

Linda pushed her plate aside and reached for her coffee cup as they approached. She eyed them uncertainly, frowning a little.

Windy swept his hat from his head. 'We'd like to speak to you, Mrs. Farrow.'

'I don't speak to the hired help,' she said coldly. She turned to hail a passing waiter. 'Garçon! This coffee's cold!'

The waiter picked up her cup and hurried off.

Windy was losing patience. 'Ma'am—'

She fixed him with icy stare. 'I see you've taken a bath. But it hardly qualifies you for this rude impertinence—'

'Shut up an' lissen for a change,' Windy growled, sliding into a chair across from her. Long Jim sat down between them.

Mrs. Farrow drew back in her chair and turned to the waiter coming back with her coffee.

'These ruffians are annoying me. I want you to throw them out!'

The waiter set her cup down and looked at Windy and Long Jim. He was a long-necked, watery-eyed man who started every morning cursing the day he had come to Goliath.

Windy drew his longbarreled Frontier and laid it on the table.

'*Vamos,*' he growled.

The waiter gulped and went away.

Mrs. Farrow started to get up. Long Jim reached out and pulled her back down.

She faced them angrily, a cold, unfrightened look in her eyes.

'When my husband gets back—'

'He's not coming back!' Windy cut her off bluntly. 'That's what we came to tell you. He left last night on the northbound stage.'

She stiffened. 'Left . . . ?'

'Bag an' baggage, as they say, ma'am.' Long Jim's voice was gentle.

She stared at them, a flicker of uncertainty in her gaze.

'But . . . he couldn't—'

'Reckon he did, Mrs. Farrow.' Windy took out the note Snopes had given him and handed it to her.

'That yore husband's handwritin', ain't it?'

She read the message, taking more time than she should have before she handed it back. Her eyes were shadowed now.

'Yes . . . I believe so—' But there was no real assurance in her voice.

Windy frowned.

She settled back in her chair. 'Then you *are* Quincy's uncle?'

'Like I told you, ma'am.'

She looked them over again and shook her head. 'Quincy didn't tell me you'd be here.'

'He didn't know I was coming,' Windy said.

The girl was silent for a moment. 'I . . . I don't know what to do now.'

'Leave on the morning stage,' Windy said.

A spot of color came into her cheeks. 'No. I won't leave until I hear from Quincy.'

'If you hear from him,' Windy said grimly.

'If?' Her face was cold. 'What do you mean?'

'I think yore husband's in trouble,' Windy said bluntly. 'He was out hunting rocks and probably stumbled onto something he shouldn't have.'

Long Jim added, 'They killed his partner, Mrs. Farrow—Bill Sawyer.'

'Bill's dead?' It slipped out and then Linda Farrow bit her lip. 'Quincy wrote me about his working with Sawyer—'

Windy said, 'There's nothing you can do here, ma'am. Me an' Long Jim would feel better if you left Goliath in the morning.'

She stiffened. 'Are you trying to run me out of town?'

Windy eyed her, exasperated. 'We're just trying to keep you out of trouble!'

Her shoulders straightened in haughty defiance. 'Why should I believe you? Quincy never once mentioned an Uncle John to me. For all I know that note is a fake—'

'You said it was his handwriting.'

'I could be wrong.' Her lips tightened. 'I'm not leaving Goliath until I hear from my husband.'

Windy rose. 'Ma'am,' he said slowly, 'yo're the stubbornest female I've had the misfortune of meeting. If Quincy married you, I'm sorry for him.' He turned to Long Jim.

'Let's go.'

Linda Farrow settled back and watched them leave, a cold and speculative light in her green eyes.

CHAPTER FOURTEEN

Chris Rader slumped in a chair, his eyes pained slits against the lamplight, and slowly shook his aching head.

'Didn't get a good look at him,' he said. 'Small feller . . . said he was looking for Harry. Sure fooled me.'

Paul Incalis paced the floor of his office. 'Two of them, you say?'

The crestfallen guard nodded. 'Must have been. Didn't see the man who hit me at all.'

The newspaperman turned an angry gaze to Jip Jensen, slouched against the wall.

'I thought you were keeping an eye on those two saddle bums,' he accused.

The deputy's eyes glittered coldly. 'You told me to leave them alone.'

'I didn't want them killed in town!' Paul snapped. 'Especially after they brought in Bill Sawyer.' He paused behind his desk, banging his right fist into the palm of his left hand. 'Damn it, Jip . . . we can blame Sawyer and Farrow on El Porcito. But—'

Chris said hopefully, 'Mebbe they didn't get to see what was in the wagon.'

'Sure,' Paul said with heavy sarcasm, 'they risked getting shot just for the hell of it, eh?'

Chris slumped deeper into his chair.

The newspaperman turned his attention

109

back to Jensen. 'Did you check on them?'

Jensen nodded. 'Snopes said they went up to their room right after I saw them in front of the barbershop and stayed there until a few minutes ago. They stopped in the hotel dining room to speak to Mrs. Farrow an' left.'

'*Mrs. Farrow?*'

Paul leaned on his desk, his knuckles whitening, and stared at the deputy. 'You mean Quincy Farrow's wife is in town?'

Jensen looked surprised. 'Came in on the westbound stage a little while ago. Real looker. I thought you knew.'

'*Christ!*' Paul Incalis sank slowly in his chair and laid his head on his folded arms. Jensen and Chris stared uneasily.

After a moment Paul raised his head. 'Fifty rifles,' he said bleakly. 'If they took a close look at them everything I've planned goes up in smoke.'

Chris said uneasily, 'Hell, they'd have to know what to look for, Mr. Incalis.'

The newspaperman rose to his feet. His voice was cold. 'I figgered them for saddle bums. Even believed the small one when he said he was Quincy's uncle. Thought they'd look around, get discouraged, and leave.'

Jensen said grimly, 'You should have let me deal with them, Paul.'

'You tried twice,' Paul sneered.

Jensen flushed angrily. 'That pint-sized galoot tricked me the first time!'

110

'And I had to get you out of a hole the second time,' Paul reminded him. He frowned. 'They look old enough to be sitting out the rest of their years in some old folks' home,' he muttered. 'Border drifters, looking for a handout. But they're tricky, and they're fast with a gun.'

He was silent a moment, thinking things out. 'They could be from the United States Marshal's office. Maybe Quincy got word back to them before—'

'Hell, you picked up Farrow's letter from his suitcase,' Jensen reminded him. 'Don't think he would have been so anxious for the Mex kid to get it over to the post office in Palmer if he had sent word before.'

Paul nodded. 'Maybe you're right.' He started to pace again. 'Can't take any more chances, though. I'll be driving the wagon myself, tomorrow.'

Chris said, 'You want them two jaspers out of the way, Mr. Incalis?'

Paul eyed him. 'Tonight?'

Chris nodded. 'I owe them something.' He touched the lump on his head.

Paul considered. 'It's got to look like an accident. I don't want to get fouled up in an investigation.'

Jensen frowned. 'Accident?'

Chris suddenly ginned. 'Sure.' He turned to the deputy. 'Old trick I learned in a logging camp, Jip. Need yore help, though.'

111

Jensen grinned wolfishly. 'I've been itching all day for a crack at them,' he said.

Paul said sharply, 'Remember, no slip-ups!'

Chris joined the deputy by the door. 'Foolproof,' he said. 'Don't you worry none, Mr. Incalis.'

Paul settled back in his chair after they left. *Foolproof!* The whole scheme he had spent months planning had seemed so. Now he wasn't so sure.

Then he remembered Mrs. Farrow. He got up, took his hat off the hook and went out.

* * *

Linda Farrow stood by the window of her room listening to the noises of the town, but not really hearing them. She had come to Goliath expecting to meet with Quincy Farrow and Bill Sawyer—but she had come a few days too late.

She looked different standing there—a tall, capable woman with no softness in her face now.

After a moment she went back to her dresser and began to brush her hair.

The knock on her door was half expected. 'Yes,' she said. 'Who is it?'

She was thinking of Windy and Long Jim, but the man outside said, 'Paul Incalis.'

She paused, hairbrush poised by her cheek, a small and startled light in her eyes.

'Oh!' There was surprise in her voice, and some confusion. 'I'm sorry, but I don't know—'

Paul opened the door and stepped inside. She could see him in the mirror, a pleasant-looking, well-groomed man.

He said, 'I don't wish to disturb you, Mrs. Farrow. But my desk clerk just informed me you were here.' He smiled. 'I didn't know Quincy's wife was coming to Goliath.'

She turned slowly to face him. 'You know my husband?'

'Quite well.' Paul closed the door. 'I run the town newspaper. I also own this hotel.'

'Oh!' Relief pouted her pretty lips. 'I'm so glad you came. Perhaps you can tell me why my husband isn't here to meet me?'

Paul shrugged. 'I'm sorry, Mrs. Farrow. Your husband left last night. Seemed to be in a bit of a hurry.' He smiled. 'Perhaps if you had let him know—'

'Oh, but I did,' she cried. She got up, her hands clenching nervously around her hairbrush. 'I wrote to him before I left.'

'Then it's quite possible your letter went astray,' Paul said. 'Postal service along the border isn't too reliable these days. El Porcito, you know—'

She stared at him. 'El Porcito?'

'A Mexican bandit across the border. There's no doubt he or some of his men killed Bill Sawyer. Must have frightened your husband, I would say.'

'Bandits?' Linda Farrow sank down on the edge of her bed. 'I thought . . . these were just wild stories invented by hack writers—'

'I'm afraid in this case they're true,' Paul said. He was watching her closely. 'Your husband ever tell you what he was doing here?'

'Studying geologic formations . . . something like that.' Her lips quivered and there was a desolate look in her face. 'I don't know what to do, Mr. Incalis. It's not like Quincy to leave me stranded.'

'You can stay here, if you wish,' Paul said, 'as long as you like. My guest, of course.'

She smiled at him through eyes that were wet with unshed tears. 'I'd like to. I'm sure Quincy will get in touch with me—' Then a shadow crossed her face. 'But . . . I'm afraid I must leave tomorrow.'

'Why?' Paul's tone was sharp.

'I . . . I've been threatened. Tonight . . . in the dining room.'

Paul strode to her. 'Someone in my employ?'

'I don't know. Two men . . . old enough to be my father. One of them claimed he was Quincy's uncle. He told me to leave on the morning stage.'

Paul's gaze narrowed. 'I think I know who you mean, Mrs. Farrow. Border ruffians . . . they don't belong in Goliath. I wouldn't be surprised if they were mercenaries in the employ of El Porcito himself.'

Linda shuddered.

'On the other hand,' Paul said quietly, 'he could be your husband's uncle, Mrs. Farrow.'

Her head jerked up. 'That's impossible. I know all of Quincy's relatives. He's an imposter!'

A gleam sifted into Paul's eyes. 'I'm sure he is, Mrs. Farrow.' He patted her on the shoulder. 'You're a beautiful woman,' he said. 'Quincy is a lucky man.'

She smiled gratefully. 'I feel better now, knowing you. Most of the men here are so . . . so uncouth—'

He smiled. 'I'd like to show you the town, Mrs. Farrow. But I have to leave early—a business trip. Perhaps when I get back?'

She nodded.

He walked to the door. 'And I wouldn't worry about those two men, Mrs. Farrow.'

'Linda,' she said. Her smile was inviting.

He paused. 'They'll be taken care of tonight, Linda.' He bowed in his most gracious manner and left.

Linda waited until he had gone down the stairs into the lobby. Then she went to the door and locked it. She stood there, hard and reflecting . . . then pulled up her skirt and carefully checked the loads in the seven-shot .22 caliber derringer in the holster strapped to her thigh!

CHAPTER FIFTEEN

The Red Bucket Saloon was crowded. Most of the talk inside was about the Mexican bandits just across the border, in the town the Americans jokingly called Todos Por Niente, but which the Mexicans knew as San Juan.

For a long time El Porcito and his ragged raiders had been little more than a joke here. But now worry had come to Goliath and the other smaller settlements scattered along the border—a worry fanned by the *Border Inquirer* and Paul Incalis's fiery editorials.

Windy and Long Jim sat quietly at a table close to the saloon doors. The batwings fanned almost continually as men went in and out.

Windy poured himself a generous slug and Long Jim eyed the rapidly diminishing whiskey in the bottle.

'Hey,' he said peevishly, 'take it easy with this rotgut. Jest because I'm buying—'

Windy scowled as he pushed the bottle toward his partner.

'I'm worried about that gal,' he said.

'Quincy's wife?'

'If she is his wife,' Windy growled. 'She wasn't sure about my nephew's handwriting. And why should a gal like her come to this border town now? Without telling her husband. Don't make sense, Jim.'

'Most women don't,' Long Jim opined sagely, 'when it comes to follerin' their hearts.'

Windy eyed him with thinly veiled skepticism. 'Where 'ud you hear that?'

'Heard it on the stage . . . up in Denver. Yuh should have been there. Some Shakespeare acting feeler.' Long Jim shook his head, still marveling at the memory. 'Man, he sure made a believer outa me—'

'That ain't hard!' Windy snapped, 'seeing as how you'll believe about anything—'

He paused as the batwings swung open and Chris Rader lurched inside. The tall man's gaze ranged over that crowded room and held briefly on the two oldsters. He turned his head away, hiding the quick gleam that came into his eyes.

He took another unsteady step forward, planted his feet wide and brushed the back of his hand across his mouth.

'Anybody seen that goddamn deppity, Jensen?'

The bartender shook his head. A chorus of 'no' greeted him from the crowd. Chris turned and staggered outside.

Windy frowned. 'What was that all about?'

Long Jim knuckled his jaw. 'That feller look familiar to you, Windy?'

The pint-sized oldster scratched his head. 'Yeah—kinda.' He looked toward the batwings, trying to place the man, and finally shrugged.

Long Jim poured himself a drink.

'We got two ways to go,' he growled, his voice not carrying beyond their table. 'We kin ride up to Palmer an' try talking to an honest lawman about what we saw in that wagon. Or we kin ride out and start looking around that El Rojo peak again, on the long chance yore nephew might still be out there an' alive.'

Windy nodded. 'I say we head back for the border country, Jim.' His eyes were hard. 'I got a hunch we won't find anybody in Palmer willing to buck the *Border Inquirer*—not without more proof than we got, anyway.'

He finished his drink and settled back, growling, 'Damn that fool nephew of mine! If only I could be sure he had come back to town an' taken that stage—'

He cut himself off as the batwings slapped open and the straw-haired deputy, Jensen, strode inside. The lawman gave them a passing glance, but moved on to the bar, where he elbowed a place for himself.

Windy scowled. 'Now that's funny.'

'What's funny?'

'Thet loud-mouthed deppity. Saw us here an' didn't say a word . . . an' him telling us earlier to stay in our room.'

'Hell, mebbe he's got other things on his mind,' Long Jim growled. 'We ain't bothering him.'

'Not yet,' Windy muttered, but his hand slid down to his holstered Colt and there was a cold and watchful glitter in his blue eyes.

'Cripes, leave the pore fool alone,' Long Jim said. There was a grin on his face. 'He was only doing his job. 'Sides, you can't rightly blame the man for not giving us the keys to the city, after what you did to him, Windy.'

'Just the same, I'm gonna keep an eye on him.' Windy settled back and took out his corncob.

'You gonna smoke that thing in here?' Long Jim demanded. But Windy ignored him. Long Jim sighed and moved his chair a bit further away.

Jensen ordered a beer and turned on his elbow, his gaze slanting coldly to the two men by the door. Then he turned back to the bartender as the man said, 'Chris Rader was in here looking for you, Jip.' The bartender shook his head. 'Drunk as a lord, he was—and he sounded mean.'

Jensen shrugged. 'Ain't my worry.' He blew off the head of his beer and took a swallow and slowly placed his glass back on the bar.

Windy, watching, said thinly, 'Keep an eye on him, Jim—'

But he turned quickly as the batwings flapped open again and Chris Rader staggered into the room. He braced himself on unsteady feet, looked around the room and spotted Jensen at the bar.

He said loudly, 'Hey, you!' Then, as Jensen turned, he shook his fist at the lawman. 'I ben lookin' all over town for you.'

Jensen gave him a look and turned back to his beer. Rader walked unsteadily to the bar and grabbed Jensen by the shoulder, pulling him around.

'Don't turn yore back on me, damn you! I ain't no—'

Jensen shoved him away. 'Go on home!' he said coldly.

Windy and Long Jim watched with narrow-eyed, skeptical curiosity.

'Not before you pay me the twenty bucks you owe me,' Rader snarled. He turned and appealed to the crowd. 'Don't think much of a man who won't pay his gamblin' debts.'

Jensen said sharply, 'Shut up, you fool!'

Rader swung clumsily around to face him. 'I want my money! Jest because you wear a badge don't give you the right to cheat—'

Jensen slapped his face. Rader staggered back and went for his Colt. The lawman's fingers closed around his wrist and he twisted the gun away from Rader, then backhanded him across the mouth.

'Now get out of here!' Jensen said grimly, 'before I kill you!'

Rader brushed his hand across his mouth. His lower lip was bleeding.

'Damn you!' he snarled. 'I'm not goin' to let you get away with this.'

He staggered outside, the batwings flapping behind him.

Jensen turned and slid Rader's gun across the bar to the bartender.

'Keep this for him,' he said. 'Don't give it back until he sobers up.'

The bartender nodded and slipped the gun under his counter.

Windy nudged his partner under the table. 'Smell something, Jim?'

Long Jim eyed the corncob sending up smoke signals from the smaller man's mouth.

'Only that manure burner yuh got choking up the place,' he said disgustedly.

'That drunk. Give yuh odds of five to one he's wearing an egg-sized lump under his hat.'

Long Jim settled back, frowning. 'The galoot I slugged in the backyard of the *Border Inquirer*?'

He started to turn toward the batwings. 'I didn't get a good look at him, but—'

'I did,' Windy said. 'Jest came back to me.'

Both men turned their attention to the bar. Jensen was hunched over his beer, but he didn't seem interested in drinking it.

There was a stumbling series of steps outside. Windy's eyes flashed a quick warning to Long Jim, who nodded.

The batwings slammed open and Chris Rader stood framed in the opening, a rifle leveled in his hands.

'All right, Jensen!' he shouted. 'I told yuh I'd be back.'

Windy and Long Jim were watching the

121

deputy. He had his back to the door, but he had been expecting this. He whirled as Rader's voice reached him, stepping clear of the bar line, his hand flashing to his gun . . .

But the muzzle, clearing its holster, swiveled around toward the table by the door!

Windy and Long Jim dove for the floor.

Jensen's first slug ripped a wicked gash at the edge of the table where Windy had been sitting and ploughed into the wall behind. His second scoured the surface where Long Jim would have been a sitting duck.

Windy rolled and came up in a crouch as Jensen swung his Colt around in a shocked, desperate move to target him. The grizzled oldster's Frontier boomed and the slugs drove the deputy back into the bar while men on both sides of the counter scattered in panic.

The deputy hung there for a shocked moment, then fell forward on his face, still clutching his Colt.

Chris Rader seemed frozen by the misplay. It took him a few seconds to recover, then he swung his rifle around. Windy and Long Jim's slugs spun him around, the rifle flying out of his grasp. He staggered for real this time and fell against the batwings and rolled out on the walk. He tried to get up and then the life went out of him and he went limp.

The silence came back into the room, shocked and unreal. Men sat frozen in their chairs, watching the two old reprobates as they backed against the wall by the batwings, long-barreled Colts leveled and deadly.

'You all saw it,' Windy said. His voice—was a rasp, low and deadly. 'Made a big play outa it. But Jensen was gunning for *us*, not him!'

No one said anything.

Slowly the two men backed to the door.

'I wouldn't advise any of you to make a move,' Windy said and Long Jim nodded grimly. 'Not for a long while, anyway!'

No one in that room did.

CHAPTER SIXTEEN

Linda Farrow was in her husband's room, now occupied by Windy and Long Jim, when she heard steps in the hallway. She had been going through Windy's warbag which she had spread out on the bed. She was holding the creased letter Windy had received from his sister, but she had no time to read it.

She froze as someone began pounding on the door across the hall.

Windy's voice had an urgent ring to it: 'Mrs. Farrow!'

She crossed to the door and opened it a crack and saw Windy and Long Jim standing by her door.

Long Jim muttered, 'She ain't in. And we ain't got time to go looking for her.'

'Can't leave her here!' Windy snapped. 'Got to get her out of town!'

He began to bang on the door again. Long Jim pulled him away. 'They won't bother her. But they sure as hell will stretch our necks if they get their hands on us, Windy, with that newspaperman, Paul Incalis, leading the parade!'

Windy backed off, thinking this over. 'All right,' he growled, 'you get the cayuses. I'll get our warbags.'

Long Jim hurried down the stairs. The girl

flattened against the inner wall as Windy turned to the door. He came into the room in a hurry, pausing by the bed as he saw his personal belongings spread out before him.

Linda came up quickly, shoving him hard from behind, sending Windy sprawling across the bed. He rolled over and reached for his gun when the sharp bark of a .22 sent him ducking between the bed and the wall.

When he poked his head up, his gun leveled, the room was empty. He ran to the hallway and looked out, but there was nothing to see. He cursed silently and went back into the room, pausing to sniff the air as a strange odor trickled into his awareness.

Wheeling, he went back across the hall and tried Mrs. Farrow's door. But it was locked and no one moved inside.

Baffled, he went back into his room and got his and Long Jim's things together.

Long Jim was waiting at the hitchrack, horses saddled and ready.

'What in hell took you so long?'

Windy glanced back into the hotel. 'Somebody was in our room, going through my bag.'

He mounted alongside his partner. 'Smelled perfume in the room. Must have been my nephew's wife.'

Long Jim scowled. 'What would she be looking for?'

'Don't know,' Windy growled. 'Ain't got

time to find out.'

They wheeled away from the hotel and left Goliath at a gallop, heading south.

From her window overlooking the street Linda Farrow watched them leave. The letter she had found in Windy's warbag told her what she wanted to know about him. Now, all she had to find out was what was in the wagon in the *Border Inquirer* shed.

*   *   *

Paul Incalis stared at Jensen's body, a bitter anger in his eyes. The room was quiet; everyone was watching him. He turned slowly and pinned his cold gaze on the bartender.

'How did it happen, Nate?'

Something inside Incalis, the edge of a growing fear, brought a thin sweat to his face. He was thinking that Jensen was no slouch with a gun . . . and the deputy had come prepared for this one!

The bartender was still badly shaken. The men in the saloon looked on, uneasy and silent.

'Looked like a shootout between Jensen and Chris Rader,' Nate said. 'Chris came in here looking for Jensen . . . claimed the deputy welched on a gambling debt. Could hardly stand, he was so drunk—'

'I don't know about that,' someone said. He was a young clerk named Simpson and he worked in Robland's General Store. 'I went

126

out to see if Rader was still alive.' He shook his head. 'If he was drunk when he came in here, the whiskey sure didn't stay with him. I even smelled his breath.'

'Hell, I don't care what you smelled,' Nate said angrily. He appealed to the others. 'You all saw Chris when he came in. Sure looked drunk to me—'

'I don't give a damn if he was drunk or not!' Paul snapped. 'I want to know who killed Jensen!'

'A little runt,' the bartender said, shaking his head. 'An' old man, graying, like a spavined mule . . . didn't seem lively enough to swat a fly. His partner, a stringbean sort of feller, got Rader.'

'You mean they just up and shot Jensen and Rader?' Paul's eyes narrowed. 'That's murder.'

'No,' the bartender muttered. 'That's the strange part of it, Mr. Incalis—'

'What in hell are you talking about? Jensen's dead. So's Rader.'

The bartender poured himself a shot of whiskey with a shaky hand and gulped it.

'Can't rightly call it murder, Mr. Incalis. Rader came back with a rifle and it looked like he was gunning for Jensen. Jensen whirled around and started shooting . . . *but not at Rader!*' He took a deep breath. 'Don't see how Jensen could miss by that much, unless he meant to. He didn't shoot at Rader—he was shooting at them two old saddle bums.'

The newspaperman stood still, waiting. Then, as Nate reached for the whiskey bottle again, he snapped, 'What do you mean, miss?'

The bartender pointed. 'Them two saddle bums were sitting right there, next to the door: They moved mighty fast when Jensen swung around. Don't know how they did it, but they hit the floor just before the deputy started shooting.'

He looked around, sweating a little under Paul's angry stare. 'I swear that's the way I saw it, Mr. Incalis.'

There was a mutter of general agreement from the rest of the men in the saloon.

Paul Incalis stood there, looking down at Jip Jensen's body, cursing the man inwardly. He had lost his best man on a play that had backfired, and now the two men responsible were loose and could be trouble. But maybe, it occurred to him, he could salvage something out of what had happened.

'All right, Nate . . . I believe you. But those two drifters killed an officer of the law tonight. That's one thing we can't let them or anyone else get away with.'

He swung around to face the men in the saloon. 'I'm posting a reward for them right now. One thousand dollars each, and don't bother to bring them back alive.'

No one moved.

He ran his gaze over them, his voice cold, disappointed: 'Well . . . ?'

128

A few men edged slowly toward the door. But they were in no hurry, remembering the way Jensen and Rader had died.

CHAPTER SEVENTEEN

Shining through a cloud, the moon cast a smoky light over the old presidio overlooking San Juan. The fire had been put out, but the stable was gutted and the sharp smell of smoke still hung over the old parade ground.

A small cluster of men watched Maria standing stiff and defiant, her hands tied behind her, around the middle execution post.

El Porcito watched from saddle of his big white stallion. Ramon waited beside him. It had taken all day to round up the scattered horses.

El Porcito's voice was cold. 'If we do not return before the sun sets tomorrow, shoot her!'

Tomas stood a few feet away from Maria, holding his shotgun. There were seven or eight other men standing around . . . only three of these had rifles. The bandoliers they wore across their chests were mostly for show—they held no cartridges.

Maria spat at the mounted man. 'Yes, shoot me, El Generale! That's all your revolution means. Shooting old men and women . . . and boys!'

El Porcito's face whitened. 'Sometimes I wonder,' he said bitterly, 'if I have spent my life foolishly, trying to free people like you

130

from bondage.'

'Bondage? Hah! What's that?' She turned to the big cantina owner.

'Slavery,' Tomas said harshly.

She leaned forward as much as the rope binding her allowed, her blazing eyes fixed on the man beside El Porcito.

'You hear that, Ramon? He wants to free us from slavery.' She began to laugh, but there was an edge of fear in her defiance.

Ramon's face was tight, his cheekbones highlighted in the moonlight. He didn't say anything.

Maria turned to the Mexican leader. 'I am nobody's slave, El Generale. But these men . . . my husband . . . you have made slaves of them. See how they obey you! Not one of them dares—'

Tomas took a threatening step toward her. 'Perhaps a gag will stop your wagging tongue, Maria!'

'Leave her be,' El Porcito said coldly. 'Soon only the wind and the coyotes will be listening to her.'

He turned to Ramon. 'Pray that nothing has gone wrong, Ramon. Or you will never see your wife again!'

Ramon nodded stiffly. 'I told you I'd be responsible for the boy. I'm ready to take the consequences of his escape.'

'Oh, you will!' El Porcito cut in harshly. He spat into the dust at his feet. 'I should have shot him, like I wanted—'

'Perhaps we are making too much of him,' Ramon said. 'It's quite possible he knows nothing of our plans of the guns that have been promised.'

'Yes,' Maria cried. 'Felipe was tied to his bed, like an animal. Can you blame him for trying to escape?'

'He came back and released the two old ones,' El Porcito snapped. 'That is not the work of a frightened boy!'

Ramon sighed. 'We do not know that, El Generale. No one saw him—'

'Bah!' El Porcito turned to Tomas. 'Remember . . . if we are not back with the guns and ammunition by sundown tomorrow— execute her!'

Tomas nodded. 'It will be as you ordered. But,' he took a step toward the leader, 'one man and one bullet will be enough for that. Let the rest of us ride with you, El Generale?'

El Porcito shook his head. 'No. It is enough for Ramon and I to risk our necks. I do not trust the Señor Incalis . . . but I must take the chance.'

He swung around to Ramon. 'Come,' he said sharply. 'I wish to be across the river before the sun comes up.'

Maria strained against the rope, watching. She called, 'Ramon—don't leave me!' And now there was a haunting fear in her voice.

He turned to look back to her, an emptiness

inside him. Strange, he thought almost emotionlessly, despite her sharp tongue he still loved her.

'I'll be back,' he promised.

She watched them ride off, El Porcito and Ramon, her eyes beginning to fill with tears.

Tomas said softly, 'You better pray, Maria, that he will!'

*   *   *

Quincy's cabin loomed up in the night, a blob of a shadow against the sloping hillside. Clouds flitted across the low-hanging moon. A coyote slunk away from the door, pausing to look back toward the sound of approaching riders. Then, suddenly frightened, it scatted away like a darting shadow.

A few moments later Windy and Long Jim rode up to the cabin and dismounted.

Long Jim glanced back along the way they had come. 'Figger we might be having company?' But his tone was not alarmed.

Windy shrugged. 'Not less'n they've got Apache trackers.'

Long Jim looked at the cabin. 'They might guess,' he said. 'Somebody in town probably knows about this place?'

'Be a fool to think we'd come here,' Windy growled.

Long Jim chuckled. 'Lawd knows there's enough fools in Goliath. Me, I ain't gonna take

133

a chance. I figger to bed down in the brush somewhere yonder.'

Windy scratched his head. 'You got a point.'

They picketed their horses in a draw a quarter of a mile from the cabin and spread their bedrolls on the soft warm sand.

They were asleep within five minutes.

*   *   *

The night fled the desert hills as the sun poked its huge red orb over the horizon. A shadow flitted across the sand toward the sleeping men.

Windy brushed at something tickling his nose and muttered in his sleep. The tickling started again and then his sleep was shattered by an unearthly hee-hawing that brought the small man clawing up and Long Jim rolling out his blanket, reaching for his rifle!

Felipe backed off, paling as Windy's Frontier leveled at him. 'Señor Windy . . . it is me, Felipe!'

The old man scowled at him as he lowered his pistol. 'Good way to get yoreself killed,' he growled. His gaze went to the camel the boy had picketed further down the wash. 'That damn beast scared me outa ten years' growth!'

'Something did that to you already,' Long Jim jeered. He pulled on his boots and stood up.

'How'd you find us, kid?'

Felipe grinned. He pointed to Windy and said, 'He make loud noise . . . like this—' The boy gave an exaggerated imitation of the small man's snoring.

Long Jim grinned. Windy snapped, 'Don't get funny, boy. Where've you been?'

The boy suddenly looked sad. 'I go back to San Juan to see my sister. I get her in plenty trouble, señor.'

Windy scowled. 'What do you mean?'

'I help you get away. El Generale is plenty mad with her and Ramon. He tell Tomas to shoot her unless he and Ramon come back with the guns.'

Windy looked at his partner. 'Figgers,' he grunted. 'That's where that wagonload must be headed.' He turned to Felipe. 'You know where Ramon and El Porcito were going to pick up these guns?'

'Somewhere around El Rojo, I think,' the boy replied.

Windy glanced off toward the red flat mountain bulking on the horizon. 'Let's go take another look around.'

They were threading between rocks on a long slope under the bulk of the mountain when Long Jim laid a warning hand on his partner's arm. He nodded to something below.

A wagon was some distance off, moving toward the base of the mountain. A woman sat stiffly between the blocky driver and Paul Incalis.

135

Long Jim muttered, 'Looks like Mrs. Farrow.'

Windy nodded. 'Wait here,' he said quietly. 'I'm going down there and find out what's happened.'

Long Jim held his arm. 'Too dangerous. We know what he's got in that wagon, and why he's out here—'

'But we don't know where he's going,' Windy said. 'Besides, that's my nephew's wife. She might be in trouble.'

He slipped out of saddle. 'I'm going down alone. You an' the boy keep outa trouble.'

He was gone before Long Jim could stop him.

CHAPTER EIGHTEEN

Paul Incalis glanced at the girl riding stiffly between him and the driver and said, 'Keep your mouth shut, Mrs. Farrow,' and then let his gaze go out to the small man limping down the slope toward them.

The blocky driver scowled and pulled to a stop. Paul said softly, 'I'll handle him, Ben.'

Windy limped toward them, a smile breaking out over his weatherbeaten face.

'Didn't expect to see you out here, Mr. Incalis.' He turned his gaze to the girl. 'And you, Mrs. Farrow.'

Linda showed her teeth in a strained smile.

Paul said, 'What are you doing out here?'

Windy wiped sweat from his brow with the back of his hand. 'Yuh probably heard,' he grumbled. 'Me an' Jim got into trouble last night. That hotheaded deppity tried to kill us. We were sitting nice an' peaceable in the saloon—'

'I heard,' Paul said. He glanced toward the slope. 'Where's yore partner?'

'Back at that old cabin of Quincy's. I rode out for another look around an' my hoss stepped in a chuckhole—'

He paused as Paul's hand came out of his coat pocket, holding a snub-nosed .38.

'What's the matter?' Windy growled. 'Don't

you believe me?'

'Sure I do,' Paul said. He smiled coldly. 'Ben—get that cannon he's packing.'

The driver jumped down and started for the small man. Windy's hand moved toward his gun.

'I wouldn't do that,' Paul said. He held his pistol close to Linda's head.

Windy stood still and let Ben take his gun. The blocky man hefted it, whistling softly.

'Where you taking her?' Windy asked.

'To see her husband,' Paul replied. 'You might as well come along. You been looking for Quincy long enough yourself.'

He motioned ahead. 'Sorry, Mr. Harris. You walk on ahead.' He chuckled. 'It's not too far.'

Windy cursed every step of the quarter-mile he traveled. The wagon rolled just behind him, the horses snorting to the load.

They went past a small canyon and at Paul's order Windy turned sharply into a narrow gulch where the walls loomed steep, cutting off the morning sun.

They left the wagon tied to a clump of mesquite, and Ben gave the smaller man a shove. 'Little climb won't hurt you none, pop. Stay in front of us an' stop when I tell you to.'

They went up the steep, rocky climb. Paul stayed behind the girl, giving her a hand when she needed it.

A third of the way up a whiskered jasper stepped out from behind a rock. He carried a rifle in the crook of his arm.

'Where'd you find the old fossil, Paul?'

'Back there, looking for his nephew, Quincy Farrow.' The rifleman clucked unsympathetically. 'Mebbe we oughta put him out of his misery?'

'Later,' Paul said. He smiled. 'I promised him he'd see his nephew first.'

The rifleman turned and disappeared between two huge rocks that came together at the top. Ben shoved Windy forward. The opening between the boulders led into a cave in the hillside.

Windy blinked. It took a few moments for his eyes to accustom themselves to the gloom.

The cave was not entirely dark. A lantern was set on a packing case in the middle of the chamber, which was about thirty feet deep and roughly rectangular. The rocky ceiling was barely six inches above Windy's head and both Paul and Ben had to stoop inside.

Windy stared. Besides the lantern there were a half-dozen smaller wooden boxes stacked in the shadows beyond, and some longer ones which Windy guessed held ammunition and some more rifles.

The whiskered guard was staring at Linda Farrow. 'Where'ud you get her, Paul?'

'Found her snooping around the wagon last night,' Paul replied shortly. 'Claims she's Quincy's wife.' He looked around. 'Get back to the wagon,' he told Ben. 'Keep a lookout for

El Porcito. He should be showing up soon.'

Ben slipped out of the cave. Paul pushed Windy and Linda ahead of him.

'There's your husband, Mrs. Farrow,' he said flatly.

The shadowy figure sitting on the damp floor with his back to the wall hunched forward. There was enough light so that Windy could make out a young, sunbrowned man in whipcord riding britches and tan shirt. Quincy Farrow weighed one-ninety and was a foot taller than Windy, but the oldster recognized him by his nose—it was slightly out of true.

'I'll be damned,' he muttered.

Paul stood with his gun in his hand. 'Take a good look, Quincy. This is your wife, isn't she?'

The girl stood stiffly, looking down at Quincy. Quincy stared, licked his lips. 'Yes . . . of course—' He took a deep breath as Windy said, 'I'll be damned!'

'So will I, Uncle Harris.' A weak grin showed on Quincy's face. 'How'd you get into this mess?'

Windy made a tired gesture. 'Yore ma was worried about you.'

Quincy looked at Paul Incalis. 'Why did you bring them into this? They—'

'Stuck their noses in where it didn't belong,' Incalis snapped.

'Stuck my nose into what?' Windy said harshly. He had taken the shoving and the

140

pushing around, knowing that Long Jim was on the loose and would soon be taking a hand.

'Sorry you came into this blind, Uncle Harris,' Quincy said. 'Take a look at those boxes. They hold Army rifles. Ammunition, too. Mr. Incalis who runs the *Border Inquirer* has a sideline—selling Army rifles to El Porcito the Mexican revolutionary across the border. He uses this cave as a warehouse. Sawyer and I stumbled upon it a few days ago.'

'You didn't fool me with that geologist gag,' Paul sneered. 'I spotted you and Sawyer for border patrolmen the minute you appeared in Goliath. If you had kept your nose out of these hills—'

He spun around toward the entrance as Ben and the whiskered guard came in behind Long Jim. Jim had his hands clasped across the top of his head; the whiskered man's rifle prodded his back.

'Found him nosing around the wagon,' Ben said.

Paul nodded. 'Figured he'd be around.' He slipped his .38 into his coat pocket, walked to the gear stacked along the wall and picked up a round tin container.

'Had an idea I'd find a use for this blasting powder.' He brought the container to the center of the cave and set it on the packing case beside the lantern. 'We'll get the rifles and the ammo out first. Then a short fuse—'

The whiskered man chuckled callously.

Long Jim was stooped forward, a sheepish look on his face. Ben was behind him. Windy's Frontier was stuck in the driver's waistband and his own was in his fist. He had his back to the cave mouth, as did all of them except Windy, and only the oldster saw Felipe's face appear momentarily in the opening. The boy had a firecracker in his hand and a smouldering twig in the other.

Windy glanced at Long Jim and thumbed his button nose. It was an old signal between them and Jim's eyes brightened.

The firecracker rolled between Ben's feet and made a loud noise as it went off within the confines of that rocky chamber.

Ben jumped and cracked his head against the stone ceiling, cursing wildly as he fired. He shot by reflex, not seeing anything to shoot at. Before he could recover Long Jim slugged him.

The driver sagged and Jim yanked the Colt from his hand, swiveling around to freeze the others.

Windy was moving toward his nephew. The girl was backing toward the entrance.

Long Jim crouched over the unconscious Ben and slipped Windy's Frontier from his waistband. He straightened, twin muzzles backing his cold order. 'Drop that rifle, mister!'

The whiskered gent dropped the rifle. Felipe darted in and picked it up, his face turning to Long Jim for approval.

'Good boy,' Long Jim said. 'Easy, ma'am,' he said sharply to the girl. 'I ain't sure about you.'

She paused a few feet away.

Windy cut Quincy free. 'Get out,' he said quickly. 'Take yore wife with you!'

Quincy started to say something, but Windy pushed him away. 'Get going!'

Quincy grabbed Linda by the arm and pulled her with him as he went out.

Windy stopped beside Jim and took his frontier from the tall man's hand. 'You, too, Jim,' he said. 'Take the boy, too.'

Jim said, 'Dammit, Windy—'

But the small man shoved him away. 'Get out!' he snapped. 'Fast!'

Long Jim ran in a crouch, scooping Felipe up as he went. Quincy and the girl were already outside.

Ben came to life then, rolling over and making a grab for Windy's legs. The oldster slashed the Colt across his head and the man slumped down.

Paul Incalis made a break for his .38. Windy's shot spun him around. The whiskered guard broke for the stacked boxes. Windy was backing toward the cave mouth. He snapped a shot into the chamber as he ran out.

It was a blind shot. The heavy slug smashed the lantern and punched a hole in the powder tin.

There was a moment of almost complete blackness. Then a bluish yellow flame licked up around the spilled kerosene . . . and the cave went up in one giant blast!

Windy was halfway down the slope, but even then the force of the explosion sent him tumbling. Behind him the hill shook and rocks rattled in a dust-raising slide.

Quincy and Long Jim hauled Windy to his feet.

'Hurt?' Quincy asked solicitously.

'Not enough to talk about,' Windy growled. He looked back up the slope and Quincy said, 'It will take a week to dig them out of there. And I don't expect to find any of them alive.'

Long Jim shook his head. 'I ain't doing any digging until I eat—hey!' he yelled, making a grab for Felipe.

The boy was holding a firecracker in his hand, his eyes bright with anticipation.

'Damn it,' Windy grumbled, 'ain't we had enough noise for one day?'

Linda was standing beside the wagon, pale but unhurt. Windy waved to her. 'There's yore wife, Quincy. Stubbornnest gal I ever—'

'She ain't my wife,' Quincy said. He smiled as he went to her. 'Not that I haven't asked her.' He went to her. 'Hello, Linda?'

She sagged against the wagon. 'This is the last time I take this kind of assignment,' she said. 'Too many damn fools running around.'

Quincy turned to his open-mouthed uncle.

'Linda works for the border patrol, same as I do.'

*   *   *

They waited by the wagon until Ramon and El Porcito showed up.

'Here's yore rifles,' Windy said. He was standing by the tailgate, a rifle in his hands. Jim was at the other corner, a rifle in his. Lounging against a rock beyond them Quincy and Linda watched, also armed. The boy was with them.

El Porcito stiffened. 'Ah,' he said bitterly, 'I told you, Ramon. That boy—'

'Probably saved yore hide!' Windy growled, 'like he saved ours. You oughta give him a medal.'

El Porcito sneered. 'A medal, señor?'

Windy threw back the canvas from the long wooden boxes. 'Fifty brand-new rifles, El Porcito. We jest checked them. All of them with faulty firing pins.'

Ramon said, 'How can that be? They are new—'

'Check them yourself,' Quincy said. He came up, pulled one out of the box and handed it to Ramon. 'Someone worked on that firing pin with a file. All of them are like that.'

El Porcito looked confused. 'Why?'

'Simple enough, if you knew Paul Incalis,' Quincy said. 'You make the raid on Goliath

145

with guns that won't shoot, and he waits for you with his own armed men. When it's over he's a bloody hero, the savior of the border towns, and one big long step toward the governor's chair.'

El Porcito sighed. 'Such dishonesty, señor—'

Ramon was scowling at the boy. 'You ready to come back home?'

Felipe looked at Quincy. Quincy smiled. 'Go on, Felipe. I'll be leaving here now.'

The boy turned his gaze to Windy and Long Jim. There was a wistfulness in his eyes. 'You, too?'

Windy nodded.

The boy hung his head for a moment. Then he turned and looked at Ramon. 'Will they shoot Maria?'

Racoon's jaw tightened as he turned to El Porcito. 'Not if I can help it, Felipe!'

El Porcito shrugged. 'Ah, there is much here that I do not understand. Perhaps, in time—' He nodded to Felipe.

'You promise to stay home?'

The boy looked at Windy and there was a smile in his eyes. 'Si, El Generale!'

'Come, then!' El Porcito waved toward the camel picketed beyond. 'Take that beast with you!'

The boy climbed up between the humps. El Porcito started to turn away, then paused. He looked back to the loaded wagon.

'Those rifles, Señor Quincy . . . perhaps, if I

could find some way to fix them—'

'Sorry,' Quincy said. 'Government property.'

El Porcito sighed. 'Ah, yes . . . the government.' He waited until Felipe rode the camel alongside them.

'No more tricks,' he said severely.

The boy shook his head.

They rode off, heading for San Juan. Windy and Long Jim watched until they were out of sight.

They turned toward Quincy and the girl. Quincy was holding Linda in his arms. He said, 'Uncle Harris—do you mind?' He waved them off.

Windy scowled. Long Jim pulled him away. 'Let them alone,' he said. 'If she ain't his wife now, she will be.'

They walked off a distance and Windy looked back.

His nephew was kissing Linda and doing a good job of it.

He shook his head. 'Like I said, Jim,' he growled, 'it's this younger generation—smart alecks, all of them.'